"I just wondered…what should I do about good-night kisses?"

"What?" Max replied with a scowl.

"A good-night kiss," Annie repeated. "How soon is it all right to kiss your date?"

"Don't think so much about it," Max advised brusquely. "A first kiss isn't such a big deal anymore…. Let it be spontaneous."

"Oh. Like this, you mean?" An impish smile curved Annie's mouth. She threw her arms around his neck and gave him a quick kiss on the lips.

As kisses went, it was one of the most innocent he'd ever received, but it hiked up Max's temperature more than he'd thought possible. Suddenly he didn't want Annie trying any of those innocent kisses on any man but him!

Dear Reader,

I hope the long hot summer puts you in the mood for romance—Silhouette Romance, that is! Because we've got a month chock-full of exciting stories. And be sure to check out just how Silhouette can make you a star!

Elizabeth Harbison returns with her CINDERELLA BRIDES miniseries. In *His Secret Heir,* an English earl discovers the American student he'd once known had left with more than his heart…. And Teresa Southwick's *Crazy for Lovin' You* begins a new series set in DESTINY, TEXAS. Filled with emotion, romance and a touch of intrigue, these stories are sure to captivate you!

Cara Colter's THE WEDDING LEGACY begins with *Husband by Inheritance.* An heiress gains a new home—complete with the perfect husband. Only, he doesn't know it yet! And Patricia Thayer's THE TEXAS BROTHERHOOD comes to a triumphant conclusion when *Travis Comes Home.*

Lively, high-spirited Julianna Morris shows a woman's determination to become a mother with *Tick Tock Goes the Baby Clock* and Roxann Delaney gives us *A Saddle Made for Two.*

We've also got a special treat in store for you! Next month, look for Marie Ferrarella's *The Inheritance,* a spin-off from the MAITLAND MATERNITY series. This title is specially packaged with the introduction to the new Harlequin continuity series, TRUEBLOOD, TEXAS. But *The Inheritance* then leads back into Silhouette Romance, so be sure to catch the opening act.

Happy Reading!

Mary-Theresa Hussey

Mary-Theresa Hussey
Senior Editor

Please address questions and book requests to:
Silhouette Reader Service
U.S.: 3010 Walden Ave., P.O. Box 1325, Buffalo, NY 14269
Canadian: P.O. Box 609, Fort Erie, Ont. L2A 5X3

Tick Tock Goes the Baby Clock

JULIANNA MORRIS

SILHOUETTE *Romance*

Published by Silhouette Books

America's Publisher of Contemporary Romance

To Carol R., Joan, Debbie R. and Brenda—
friends like you make each day better.

SILHOUETTE BOOKS

ISBN 0-373-19531-1

TICK TOCK GOES THE BABY CLOCK

Copyright © 2001 by Julianna Morris

All rights reserved. Except for use in any review, the reproduction or utilization of this work in whole or in part in any form by any electronic, mechanical or other means, now known or hereafter invented, including xerography, photocopying and recording, or in any information storage or retrieval system, is forbidden without the written permission of the editorial office, Silhouette Books, 300 East 42nd Street, New York, NY 10017 U.S.A.

All characters in this book have no existence outside the imagination of the author and have no relation whatsoever to anyone bearing the same name or names. They are not even distantly inspired by any individual known or unknown to the author, and all incidents are pure invention.

This edition published by arrangement with Harlequin Books S.A.

® and TM are trademarks of Harlequin Books S.A., used under license. Trademarks indicated with ® are registered in the United States Patent and Trademark Office, the Canadian Trade Marks Office and in other countries.

Visit Silhouette at www.eHarlequin.com

Printed in U.S.A.

JULIANNA MORRIS

has an offbeat sense of humor, which frequently gets her into trouble. She is often accused of being curious about everything...her interests ranging from oceanography and photography to traveling, antiquing, walking on the beach and reading science fiction.

Julianna loves cats of all shapes and sizes, and last year she was adopted by a feline companion named Merlin. Like his namesake, Merlin is an alchemist—she says he can transform the house into a disaster area in no time flat. And since he shares the premises with a writer, it's interesting to note that he's particularly fond of knocking books onto the floor.

Julianna happily reports meeting Mr. Right. Together they are working on a new dream of building a shoreline home in the Great Lakes area.

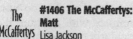

Chapter One

A car pulled into the parking area of the store, and Annie James's eyes widened as she recognized the driver.

"Max Hunter," she breathed.

A quiver of awareness went through her body, no matter how hard she tried to stop it. Okay, so it was Max. She still lived next door to his grandmother, so there was nothing remarkable about seeing him, especially now that he'd moved back to California.

"Nothing," she assured herself. He might be the most attractive man she'd ever known and sent tingles down her spine with his smile, but they were just friends.

Max helped an elegantly clad woman from his BMW, and Annie bit her lip. It was a good thing she'd accepted that Max was Max and that he preferred sophisticated city women, not small-town girls more comfortable in T-shirts than silk blouses. She just wasn't his type. Problem was, she didn't seem to be any man's type.

"Stop that, Barnard." Annie absently pulled a ledger book away from the large brown rabbit chewing on the corner.

His velvety nose twitched, and he hopped until he could sink his teeth into the paper again.

"Silly thing."

Annie stroked his soft fur and sighed. The usual Saturday bustle of a farm-supply store revolved around her, and here she was, talking to a rabbit.

She had to get a life.

Preferably a life that included a gold ring, a baby on the way and a honest-to-goodness man in her bed every night. There was just one tiny drawback to that idea—she didn't have the slightest idea how to carry it out.

It wasn't a new thought. Having grown up with a widowed father and being firmly planted in all the local boys' minds as a "nice" girl, she didn't have much experience with the opposite sex. If she wanted to break out of that mold and get herself a husband, she needed an advisor—someone to get her through the rough spots.

Sort of a romantic guidance counselor.

She looked out the window again, an idea creeping into her mind. Actually, Max was perfect for the job. If anyone could advise her about men and what appealed to them it was Max Hunter. And since he lived in the city, he'd know about the hot spots where single people shopped, and stuff.

Somewhere in the back of Annie's mind she knew

there was a risk to the idea, but she needed to make a change, and Max seemed heaven-sent.

"Problem, boss? You're kinda distracted."

Annie looked up at her teenage warehouseman and gave her head a determined shake. "Nope. Did you get Mr. Zankowski taken care of, Darnell?"

"Yup. If he was any happier he might even crack a smile."

Mr. Zankowski was a notoriously dour safflower farmer. Rumor had it he'd smiled once when Dwight D. Eisenhower was elected president, but Annie wasn't sure she believed the story.

"Great wheels." Darnell was staring out at the parking lot. "Man, I'll never have wheels like that on minimum wage."

"You're a teenager. You aren't supposed to have wheels like that." She pulled the ledger away from the rabbit a second time and tossed it in a drawer.

"You've been talking to Mom. Do you know she makes me save *half* my paycheck for college? The half before taxes?"

"It's because she loves you." Even as Annie said the words, a pang went through her. If she didn't do something soon, she might never have her own son or daughter. It was all good and fine to be an honorary aunt to most of the kids in town, but it wasn't the same.

Darnell headed back toward the warehouse with a last, longing glance through the window. The bell over the door tinkled, and Annie looked up.

"How charming," a woman drawled. "It's so rustic." Her tone wasn't complimentary.

"You could have stayed in the car," Max said.

Annie's spirits lifted. Max really *was* perfect. He was perfect even when everyone else in high school was struggling with bad hair and worse skin. He had dark-toned skin and jet-black hair—courtesy of his Native American grandfather—a sexy smile and the brooding expression of a loner...unless you looked closely and saw the twinkle in his dark eyes. On top of everything else, he was six foot two, with the physique of an athlete.

In other words, be-still-my-heart gorgeous.

Her heart might still flutter over Max, but it was safer and smarter to ignore those feelings. And, when all was said and done, they'd remained pals while the rest of his girlfriends had gone the way of the Dodo bird. She didn't want someone that handsome, anyway. Men like Max were too complicated, too interested in a fast-paced glitzy life. Give her someone like the new schoolteacher in town and she'd be happy.

"Hey, Annie."

She stood and leaned against the timeworn front counter. "Hey, Max. What are you doing here?"

"Er, looking at some property with a client. Miss Blakely has decided to build a summer home out on the delta and wants me to design it." He rolled his eyes and gave her a private wink. "Then she got thirsty and I remembered you had a soda machine here at the store."

"Darling, I told you...please call me Buffy." The woman slid her arm into Max's with a proprietary look on her face, and a pained expression replaced his smile.

Annie choked.

Buffy Blakely?

Well, she supposed it took all kinds.

"The machine is in the back," Annie said. "Do you need some quarters?" She punched a button on the ancient cash register and the door shot open. With the ease of long practice she let it bounce against her tummy, preventing it from flying across the room.

"You don't have that fixed yet?" Max looked surprised, and she remembered earlier days when she hadn't caught the drawer in time and they'd spent the next half hour chasing quarters and nickels. Once she'd bumped into him under the desk, and she could have sworn he was about to kiss her, but it turned out she was mistaken.

"No." Annie wrinkled her nose at the faint disapproval in his eyes. "They say it's unfixable." She patted the ornate brass and polished wood of the cash register. She didn't care about the quirky drawer, she liked the old thing. It had character. Why did everyone want to get rid of lovely old things and replace them with new things that didn't have any history?

"*Max*. Must this take so long? It's so dusty in here," Buffy said, obviously miffed at being ignored.

"Why don't you wait in the car?" he suggested, removing his arm from her grasp and handing her the key ring. "I haven't seen Annie for over a month. I'd like to catch up on local news."

Buffy pocketed the keys with a tight smile. "Thanks, but I'll wait."

"Swell." Max turned back to Annie. "Grandmother mentioned how terrific you've been helping out while she had the flu, and all. I didn't know she was sick."

"Oh..." Annie said, flustered. "You've been so

busy since you moved back from Boston, she didn't want to bother you. And I was happy to help, you know that.''

That's Annie, Max thought fondly. A doer. The kind of woman who rolled up her sleeves and wasn't afraid of getting her hands dirty. She was just as kind-hearted as the day he'd moved in with his grandmother. Two years younger than him, but she'd always seemed even younger with her sweet face and earnest eyes.

If the rest of Mitchellton was like Annie, then it wouldn't be so bad. But it was just a forgotten little town on the Sacramento River delta—thirty years behind the rest of the world, moving at its own relentlessly slow pace. Mitchellton never changed; it was less than twenty-five miles from the state capital of Sacramento, but it might as well be a thousand for all it cared.

"Grace says your new architectural firm is doing great,'' Annie murmured. "She's so proud. She said you've also won several awards.''

"I'm doing all right.'' Max frowned. "I've been trying to convince Grandmother to move into Sacramento, but she keeps refusing.''

"She likes Mitchellton.''

"But I'd get her a condo with all the latest amenities. And she'd be so much closer to the best doctors and a first-rate hospital.''

Annie sighed. "This is where Grace's friends are, Max. You know that.''

"*Max,* I'm really thirsty,'' Buffy said through gritted teeth.

At the moment Max didn't care if she was on the

moon, much less thirsty, but he sighed and pinned a polite smile on his face. Some commissions weren't worth the time and trouble, and this one was definitely headed in that direction. "Of course. We'll get something out of the machine."

He caught Annie covering her mouth with her hand in a blatant attempt not to laugh and gave her a mock glare.

Damn, it was good to see her, especially with someone like Buffy the Architect Slayer in tow. In her quest for the "ideal" summer house Buffy Blakely had gone through four architects. Max suspected the previous four had all been single and in the thirty-something age range. Buffy wasn't subtle about wanting more from the relationship than a house design—she wanted to get married.

Marriage.

Max shook his head and shuddered.

Marriage was *out*. His mother and father had nine divorces under their combined belts, and he'd lost track of how many stepsiblings he'd had between them. He supposed you could argue they were optimistic to keep trying, but it wasn't for him. You didn't have to get your hand slammed in a car door to know it wouldn't feel good.

"*Max*." Buffy's tone had reached a higher pitch than he'd ever heard before, and he sighed.

With Buffy following close on his heel, he threaded his way between displays of gardening tools and vegetable seeds. In the back of the store was an ancient soda pop machine. It was the old-fashioned kind where you pulled the bottle out by the neck and the next one rolled into place. Max stopped in front of it and took his wallet from his pocket.

"That's *it?*" Buffy stared at the ancient soda dispenser as if "it" were about to attack her.

"Yeah." He dropped money into the slot. "Do you want cola, or lemon-lime? And I think there's orange, too."

She didn't say anything, just stared at him stonily, so Max selected a lemon-lime, popped the cap off and handed it to her. He knew she expected designer water or some other trendy drink, but this was Mitchellton, and he doubted they'd ever heard of designer water.

"Annie, do you want one?" he called. "My treat."

"Sure. Anything is fine."

Still ignoring Buffy and her frozen face, Max got another lemon-lime and brought it to Annie. She smiled a thank-you and took a long swallow, tipping her head back. Max watched idly, thinking it was a very graceful gesture, simple and uncomplicated.

Like Mitchellton, Annie hadn't changed much. Her face had the same sweetheart shape, dominated by big blue eyes and framed by reddish brown hair. Her smile was just as contagious as always and made you feel good just looking at it. She was as slim as ever, too, but she usually wore baggy clothing that concealed everything but the taut curve of her breasts.

Odd that she'd never gotten married. Mitchellton was a marrying kind of place, and in her way Annie was quite pretty. And, if her bust was any indication, she had a figure that would make most men ecstatic in bed.

"Is something wrong, Max?" Annie's puzzled

voice sent a jolt through him and he swallowed uncomfortably.

Where had *that* come from?

He was definitely being affected by the hot sunshine outside and the annoying presence of Buffy Blakely. Friends did not have licentious thoughts about another friend, especially when the friend was someone like Annie. She was like a kid sister, for Pete's sake.

"I was just thinking," Max said lamely. As long as she didn't ask what he'd been thinking *about,* he was okay. He certainly didn't want to embarrass her. Annie would probably turn beet-red if she thought anyone was looking at her chest.

"Oh, right. You know, there's something I've been thinking about, too, and...uh, I thought you'd be a good person to...discuss it with," she stuttered.

Max looked at her and wondered what could possibly make Annie so tongue-tied. He was about to ask, when a look of horror crossed her face.

"*No,* Tigger. Stop. Come here," she cried.

Max followed the direction of Annie's dismayed gaze and saw a large tiger-striped cat walking toward Buffy. He didn't understand at first, then he saw something was hanging from the feline's mouth.

With a pleased "marooow," Tigger dropped his gift right on Buffy's sandal-clad foot.

Time seemed frozen for a second, with three humans and a cat staring at a dazed mouse reclining on fine Italian leather.

All at once Buffy screamed and kicked out in a move that would have made the coach of the Green Bay Packers proud. The mouse flew across the room and landed on a padded dog bed. It blinked a couple of times, looked around cautiously and made a bee-line for a hole in the wall. Tigger followed in hot pursuit.

"Well...that was exciting," Max murmured.

"Exciting?" Buffy glared. "I'll probably get some horrible disease from that disgusting little rodent."

If the truth be told, Max was more worried about the mouse. It couldn't be healthy coming into such close contact with Buffy. "I'm sure you'll be fine."

"What do you know about it? Don't just stand there, get a doctor. Get some disinfectant."

One of Max's eyebrows shot upward. She sounded like Lucy in a Charlie Brown cartoon, screaming about dog cooties, and it was getting harder and harder to keep from laughing.

He cast a glance at Annie, who stood with one hand covering her mouth and her eyes opened impossibly wide. She was plainly sharing his trouble in keeping a straight face. "I think I have some iodine," she said.

That did it. Max couldn't have kept from laughing any more than he could have stopped breathing.

"You...you *monster*. I'm suing. I'm suing this re-volting store and this entire pathetic town," Buffy screeched, her carefully modulated voice turning into a cracked soprano. "And you, Mr. Maxwell Hunter, can go to hell."

Turning on her well-shod heel, she stalked out of the store, down the steps and climbed into the driver's seat of his BMW. The motor roared into life, and she peeled out of the parking lot, leaving a strip of rubber on the asphalt.

Tarnation. Max winced. That car was his baby. The first real indulgence of his success, and Buffy was treating it like a vehicle in a stock-car rally.

"Do you think she's actually going to sue?" Annie asked. She bit her lip worriedly.

"Naw." He shrugged. "Don't worry about it. She hates looking ridiculous."

"I don't know, she seemed really angry. Maybe she won't care how it looks."

Max leaned forward and tugged a lock of Annie's hair. "You're forgetting one little thing—Buffy just stole my BMW. An alleged mouse attack doesn't stack up to grand theft auto."

For a man whose car had just been taken and who'd probably lost a big design commission, Annie didn't think Max seemed too upset. Still, maybe now wasn't the best time to spring her little scheme on him. She'd take him home and feed him a meal. Then she'd drive him back to Sacramento and they could make plans on the way.

If he agreed.

On the other hand, she might just wimp out and never say anything at all.

No.

Annie set her jaw stubbornly. She'd spent her entire thirty-two years in a romantic black hole. If she didn't do something about it now, her life would never change. The thought sent a quaking sensation through her stomach. It wasn't that things were so bad, they were just...*nothing.* And now she had a deadline from the doctor to worry about.

"Do you want to make out a report to the sheriff?" she asked, picking up the receiver to the phone. "I don't suppose you want to see Buffy on the most-wanted list, but you could get it on the record."

Max grinned. "Why not? I'll give them an unofficial report on the unlikely chance Buffy decides to make trouble."

Annie dialed the number and handed the receiver to him. Their tiny little county boasted a sheriff and a part-time deputy—crime wasn't exactly a problem around Mitchellton. The delta islands were a lost corner of the world; folks tended to forget they even existed.

She listened while Max said hello to the deputy and explained the circumstances of his missing car, saying he wanted the authorities to know what had happened "just in case."

Newell didn't ask for details about the "just in case" part of Max's statement, which was exactly what Annie could have predicted. Unlike his newly elected and dedicated boss, Newell wasn't the most ambitious deputy in the world. He was happy to go along with anything that meant he could remain in the office with his feet on the desk.

When Max was finished, Annie took the phone and glanced at him from under her lashes. "I'll close the store and take you over to Grace's house," she murmured. "And I'll even fix dinner to make up for the trouble."

"Buffy is the one who made trouble," he said. "And don't close early for me. I'd appreciate the ride, but you shouldn't lose business because you're doing me a favor."

"That's all right. I don't get very many customers on Saturday afternoon." Annie walked to the door of the warehouse adjoining the store, where Darnell was stacking fifty-pound sacks of fertilizer along one wall. "I'm closing early," she called. "You can go, too."

Darnell's face brightened. "I've got a date tonight. Do I still get paid for the same time?"

"Yes."

The teenager let out a happy whoop, and in the space of sixty seconds he had the loading dock closed and was on his bike, pedaling furiously down the road.

"I used to get that excited about date night," Max said as Annie emptied the cash register and counted the money. "Remember what it was like?" he asked, a rueful smile on his mouth.

Annie pressed her lips together. Sooner or later she would have to discuss her lack of romantic experience with Max, but she would rather it was later than sooner. Besides, he knew she'd never dated during high school. She'd watched him go out with one girl after another, but Friday and Saturday nights had always meant something different for her.

"It was great," Max continued, seeming not to notice she hadn't answered his question. "Nothing to worry about except school exams and an excess of hormones. Those were the days."

"Not…really."

Max winced, hearing the strain in Annie's voice. He guessed happy times were scarce in Annie's memories—her father had gotten sick during that period, and she'd taken care of him for several agonizing years before his death.

"Sorry, Annie. I forgot. You didn't have that much fun in high school, did you?"

Her shoulders lifted in a barely perceptible shrug. "It doesn't matter."

"It matters. I guess most of us would rather forget what childhood was really like," he said soberly. "Mentally skip the bad parts."

"You always said things got better...after you came to live with Grace."

"That's for sure. A little dull, but much better than before." Max rubbed his jaw. In the end he'd almost turned into a normal kid, thanks to Grace Hunter. She'd been a calm, safe anchor in the middle of his parents' volatile, ever-changing relationships.

"If you can't provide a decent home for my grandson, I'm taking him to live with me," Grace had declared when he was eleven years old. They hadn't argued for long. He'd reached an age where he was a royal pain, full of resentment and a know-it-all-attitude. It was probably a relief when Grace hauled him off to Mitchellton.

Annie wrote some figures in a ledger book, then put the money she'd counted into a cloth bag and stuffed it into a hidden safe. Max frowned.

"Should you do that?" he asked. "Just leave it here? We can go by the night deposit at the credit union."

She shook her head. "We didn't have many cash sales today—never do on Saturdays. It'll be fine over the weekend."

He didn't like it, though he knew she must have been doing the same thing for years. Things were different in the city. You had to be a lot more careful.

But still...

"Besides, I have to be back here by seven on Monday, and I'll need cash for the day," Annie said. She wrote Closed Early on a piece of paper and taped it on the window. "There's a load of hay being delivered."

Max swallowed another protest. Annie was such a small thing, she barely came to his chin. She might be strong for her size, but that didn't mean she could handle bales of hay or other heavy lifting. A farm supply store wasn't the kind of place you expected a woman to operate, but she'd taken over after her father's death and kept the business going.

He looked around the store, seeing the racks of seeds, pet food and supplies, garden implements and a myriad of other items. Except for the pet supplies, it wasn't much different from twenty years ago. For that matter, the business probably hadn't changed in the past fifty years.

"There now, Barnard. We're going home," Annie said, reaching down and picking up a large brown rabbit from the desk. She tucked the creature under an arm and fished a small set of keys from her jeans pocket. "Ready?" she asked.

Max looked from the twitching nose of the rabbit to Annie's sweet face. Only Annie James would bring a pet rabbit to work with her.

"What about Tigger?"

"Tigger lives here in the store. He's responsible for keeping rats and mice from invading the warehouse."

Max grinned. "Yeah. And he doesn't do a bad job running off annoying customers, either."

Annie looked guiltily embarrassed, and he had a sudden urge to give her a hug. She worried too much about things. But then, she'd had to grow up quickly when her father got sick, so he supposed it was understandable.

"It's okay, kiddo," he assured softly. "Buffy was a major pain in the behind. I owe Tigger a treat for getting rid of her."

She smiled. "Get him some catnip. It makes him goofy."

Max grimaced as he followed her out the door. He was the goofy one, thinking about hugging Annie, because he had the sneaking suspicion that his desire to hug her had less to do with comfort than it did with wondering how she'd feel in his arms.

Chapter Two

"That was delicious, Annie," said Grace Hunter as she neatly folded her napkin.

"I haven't eaten this much in a month," Max groaned, spooning a last bite of rhubarb cobbler into his mouth. "I sure missed your cooking in Boston, Annie."

Annie smiled shyly. "Thank Grace, she taught me."

"Thanks, Grandma," Max said. He eyed the remains of the cobbler in the baking dish and wondered if he could find room for a second helping, then decided it was impossible.

There was nothing sophisticated about Annie's cooking, but it was good. On top of everything else, it was filled with fresh-picked produce out of her own garden—from cherry tomatoes to the herbs she'd used to season the zucchini and roasted chicken.

"I'm a little tired. Maybe I'll go home and watch

that documentary about Japan,'' Grace murmured. ''Will you stay and help Annie with the dishes, Max?''

''That's a good idea,'' he said, giving her a kiss. Normally Grace had boundless energy, and a worried frown creased Max's forehead as he watched her slowly cross the yard and go into the house next door.

''It's okay,'' Annie said quietly. ''She's still getting over the flu.''

''Are you sure? She's always been so indestructible. I've never seen her this tired.''

Annie nodded. ''She's sixty-seven, Max. It takes her longer to recover. The doctor says she'll probably live to be a hundred, but to remember she isn't a kid any longer.''

''You've talked to him?''

''Oh, yes. We've had a number of conversations.''

There was a note of steel in Annie's voice, and Max grinned. She was protective of the people she loved. No doubt she'd put the doctor on the spot more than once.

It had been a pleasant, lazy afternoon of visiting and working around the two houses. Annie had offered to take him into Sacramento, but he'd suggested they wait until the next day so he could spend more time with Grace. Lately he'd barely had time to think, much less visit Mitchellton as often as he ought to.

His grandmother called it the price of success. If he wasn't spending fourteen hours a day working on a design, he was on a plane heading for Boston, or Paris or somewhere else in the world to inspect one of his projects. It was important to see the buildings go up, to consult with the contractors and make any necessary adjustments.

And he loved it. Always busy, always on the go. A far cry from Mitchellton where the sum total of weekly excitement was going to church on Sundays and attending the Friday-night high school football game.

Max helped as Annie rinsed dishes and put leftovers in the refrigerator. There was an odd tension about her, and his brow drew together in a frown.

"I see you painted in here," he murmured, noting the pale-blue walls that once were a tired yellow.

"After Christmas. It was getting pretty bad." Annie rubbed her palms across her thighs in a nervous gesture.

She'd been edgy for hours, and Max remembered she'd mentioned having something to discuss. Obviously, it was something that made her self-conscious, and he wondered what it might be. Since she'd already reassured him about his grandmother's health, it probably wasn't about Grace.

"Let's take a walk," he suggested. "I haven't been down on the old levee for years."

"Oh…okay." Annie waited in the yard while he went into Grace's house to say they would be gone for a while. When he came out, they followed an overgrown path toward the river. Along this section of the river the road wasn't built on the levee, so there was a wide place on the top for easy walking.

Annie loved this time of the day, when the sun rested gold and mellow above the horizon and the world seemed to be holding its breath. It was still hot, but in the endless moments before sunset, the heat resonated through your body and no longer seemed an imposition. You were part of the land, knowing the evening would soon cool, but in the meantime your senses were tuned to each call of a katydid and the lazy swish of the river.

"I keep forgetting how beautiful it is here," Max commented after a long silence.

"Maybe because you couldn't wait to leave." As soon as the words were out, Annie winced. Lord, she had a big mouth.

Max looked at her. He wasn't smiling, but he didn't seem angry. "And you were only interested in staying. That was the biggest difference between us."

"It's a good place, Max. A wonderful place to raise children and make a life."

"I guess. But you've never had kids."

She should have expected him to say something like that, but it still caught her off guard. "No, I didn't." Despite her best efforts, the words came out sounding choked.

"Annie, what's wrong? You've been tense all afternoon."

She took a deep breath. It was the time to ask, but she was having second thoughts about asking Max to help her. He was too busy with his architectural firm and his city life. Anyway, how could he understand? *No one* understood.

Girls in small towns were just as experienced and sexually aware as the ones in big towns. But somehow Annie had just gotten left behind.

She dug her fingernails into the palms of her hands and tried to decide what was more important—her pride or the need to change her life.

"Come on, Annie. You can talk to me. We used to talk about everything."

Yeah, right, she thought, rolling her eyes. She adored Max, but there were times when he had the sensitivity of a brick. He didn't like talking about personal stuff, which was something she'd always respected. Over the years keeping things on a breezy, comfortable level with him had become second nature.

"Whatever it is, just say it," he encouraged. "Maybe I can help."

Annie wet her lips with the tip of her tongue. She might as well jump right in before she totally lost her nerve. "Well...actually, you *might* be some help. I, er, wondered if you'd...that is, I wondered if you'd kind of advise me about...attracting a man."

Max stared, and it looked as if his face was turning red beneath his naturally tanned skin. But she couldn't be sure. One of the great blessings of Max's Native American blood—next to his incredible good looks—was that no one could really tell if he was embarrassed enough to blush.

"You want me to...*what?*"

She took a deep breath and tried to sound very practical and reasonable. "Advise me. You know, tell me the right clothes to wear. Teach me about what kind of makeup and perfume men prefer. I could ask one of my friends, but I figure you could save time by avoiding ideas that aren't right. Maybe we could even do a...a practice date. Or something. Of course I'd pay for everything."

Max didn't say anything, just kept staring.

"Okay. We wouldn't have to do the date thing,"

Annie said hastily. "But the clothes and stuff would help. And maybe teaching me the right things to say."

"What the hell for?"

Annoyance flashed through her chest, strengthening her resolve. Why did most women want to attract a man? "I want to get married."

"Jeez." Max raked his fingers through his hair, looking more frustrated than she'd ever seen him. "Every woman I know wants to get married. They're batty about the subject. Did you all join a club?"

For the first time in her life, Annie understood why a woman would slap a man's face—it was because of his incredible denseness and stupidity.

"Forget it," she snapped.

"Now, wait—"

"No. I'm not waiting any longer. I can't."

Turning on her heel, Annie stomped down the levee. Men were insufferable. Maybe she shouldn't think about getting married. Maybe she should adopt a child. Adoption was possible. Single women were able to adopt children these days, though it was still harder than if you were married. And that was plenty hard enough.

Yet deep in Annie's heart she knew adoption wasn't what she wanted. Maybe it was selfish, but she wanted to have a baby. Life was a miracle, whether it was a baby chick breaking out of its shell, or a baby growing inside her womb. And if she didn't do something about it now she'd never be a part of that miracle.

"Annie. Stop."

Her stride faltered. In the distance was a spreading

oak tree. It grew in the rich loam of delta soil, drinking river water through its long roots, surviving even the worst of droughts. She'd cried and dreamed under that tree her entire life, and she didn't want to share it with Max, not today.

"Wait." Max caught her arm, dragging her around to a halt. "All right, I'm sorry I overreacted. Let's talk about this."

"There's nothing to talk about."

"Obviously, there is."

They faced each other, both angry in their own way. Distantly Annie remembered what she should have remembered before, that Max didn't trust marriage. He saw his parents as two people who'd spent their lives choosing and discarding spouses with less regard than most people use to buy and sell a car. But he blamed marriage for his mother and father's mistakes, not their failure to choose well.

"Just forget it," Annie said after a long moment.

She tore her gaze away from Max and stared at the river. It was a green body of water that seemed to move tranquilly through the wide channel. But it wasn't tranquil, it was a deep, strong river with currents that were deadly if you weren't careful. A lot like life, her father used to say.

"Annie..." Max murmured helplessly. "It just shocked me, especially that part about attracting a man."

Her eyes narrowed. "I'm sorry the idea of me being attractive is so shocking."

"*Dammit*. That's not what I meant. I've always thought you were pretty."

"What a wonderful affirmation of my sexual appeal."

"Will you stop twisting my words?" He reached down and grabbed a rock, flinging it as hard and fast as he could out into the river. The humor, usually so evident in his face, was missing, leaving only darkness.

Annie sighed.

This really wasn't Max's fault. And she wasn't so much angry, she was scared. The doctor said she only had a few months to make a decision about having a family. She'd always thought that someday she'd meet the perfect man and they'd start a family—like fate or karma unwinding into its proper place. But that ideal "someday" didn't have time limits, and she did.

"I don't get it," Max said, making a visible attempt at calmness. "You're an attractive woman. You must have had plenty of chances to get married."

Annie pushed her fingers inside the pockets of her jeans and shrugged. "Mitchellton is a farm community. People get married young around here. With Dad being sick and all, I never...dated much. Then later most of the guys in our class were already married or gone."

She'd almost said *never* dated, but wasn't willing to admit that much to Max. It wouldn't be easy admitting to anyone that you were a thirty-two-year-old virgin with the dating record of a nun, but it seemed worse saying it to Max. He probably had women lined up at his door, drooling at the thought of meeting him.

"Okay." Max didn't look convinced, but at least he didn't seem quite so astonished. "But this idea about me...advising you. I don't know what I could tell you.''

''Like I said, about clothes and makeup and stuff. You're a man, so you know what guys find attractive.''

Max tried to think of a gentle way to say no. He couldn't help Annie, not the way she wanted. But when he opened his mouth, the words died in his throat. In the depths of her blue eyes was a lingering unhappiness.

It reminded him, too much, of the days when she'd finally realized her father was going to die—that no matter how hard she worked, how many tempting meals she cooked for him or how long she prayed at church, he wasn't going to get better. Max hadn't been able to help Annie then, but he'd be damned if he wouldn't try now.

''What's wrong, Annie? Why the big rush?''

She swallowed, the muscles working in her throat, and he almost reached out to touch her. Instead he gathered his fingers into fists, waiting.

''Uh...well, I have a condition that needs surgery.''

It wasn't what he expected, and a sick sensation slammed through his stomach. ''Are you going to be all right?''

Annie nodded. ''I'm fine, Max. I have cysts on my ovaries. They aren't serious, at least not at the moment. But if I'm ever going to have children, I have to do something about it. *Now.* I can't wait.''

Max closed his eyes, unsure if it was relief or rage flooding his veins. Annie didn't deserve this. Of all the people he knew, she was the nicest. She was sweet and generous. Despite losing her father so young, she had a quick smile and never did anything to hurt another person.

"Is it safe, waiting?" he asked awkwardly. Annie's life was more important than her ability to have children, though he doubted she'd agree.

Her shoulders lifted, then dropped. "The doctor says it's all right for now, but I can't wait forever. I've been given a specific time frame to work with. Because after…after the surgery I might not be able to conceive."

Max could see how much the admission cost Annie. "I see. That's why there's a time limit."

"I don't know if you can understand how important this is," Annie said hesitantly. "You've never been interested in becoming a father, so it probably doesn't make sense to you."

"No, it doesn't," he said honestly. Max didn't have anything against children, but from what he'd seen, they complicated the dubious institution of marriage even more. "But try me."

Annie rubbed her arms, a distant expression on her face. "I have a good life here in Mitchellton. I'm an honorary aunt to half the kids in town. I'm an honorary member of the PTA. I've stood in as a Lamaze coach for my friends when their husbands couldn't handle it. I've even been an honorary 'sweetheart' for the men's group at church."

She stopped, and Max ached at what she'd said…and what she hadn't said. She was "honorary" everything. A stand-in. It wasn't enough, not for a woman like Annie.

"And when you go home…?" he whispered.

"I'm by myself. Except for my rabbit." Annie

gave him a smile, yet her voice shook. "I always thought there was plenty of time for things to change, but it turns out there isn't."

"The right guy wouldn't care if you couldn't have children," Max said.

Her shoulders lifted in a small shrug. "*I* care. I don't think I could marry someone, knowing he might never be a father because of me."

Max wanted to argue the point, but he didn't know what to say, and it seemed hypocritical in light of his own feelings on the subject.

"There's an alternative, of course," Annie continued. She looked uncomfortable and he frowned. "My doctor discussed it with me on my last visit. You see, I could have a child without going through the usual...process."

"The usual process?" Max repeated, then suddenly realized what she meant. An alternative—as in getting pregnant in a fertility clinic and bypassing the father's immediate role in conceiving the baby. "No. I don't like that alternative," he said immediately.

"Neither do I." She sighed and kicked a tuft of grass.

"And what does your doctor mean, discussing something like that? He's way out of line," Max continued, annoyed.

Annie chuckled and patted his arm. "*She's* just ensuring I know my choices. And I'm surprised at you. Artificial insemination is a very modern process. Why are you so shocked? You're the one who lives in the city."

"I'm not shocked."

Except he was.

The idea of Annie going to a sperm bank tied his guts in a knot. Not that she wouldn't be beautiful pregnant. Max had a brief, startling picture in his mind of how Annie would look, her tummy round with a child. Heat crawled through him, which shocked him even more.

Annie was…Annie.

A friend.

A *terrific* friend.

She helped his grandmother and reminded him of less complicated times. He could always count on her kindness and sense of humor. But even when he'd been a teenager with rampaging hormones, he'd never thought of her as a woman, except maybe in passing.

"…and it's too dangerous."

Max realized he'd missed Annie's last statement. "What's that again?"

She scowled. "I said I considered just going out to a bar and trying to seduce someone. But it doesn't feel right, and I don't know anything about seducing a man."

"So you need my help…in seducing some guy so you can get pregnant."

Max's jaw hardened. There was no way he'd let Annie sleep with a stranger. Even if he had to follow her to a singles bar every night, she wasn't going home with anyone. And he'd punch any guy who tried to get lucky. As a matter of fact, he wasn't too thrilled to think of Annie sleeping with *anyone*—but a stranger was definitely out.

"*Max.*" Annie fixed him with a stern gaze. "You aren't listening. I want to fall in love. I want my child to have a mother *and* a father. Sheesh. I asked you to help me find a husband, not do anything question-able. Believe it or not, a lot of men want to get mar-ried and have a family. It isn't that unusual.''

"Oh. Yeah, right.'' The shock of it all was getting to him, turning his normally clear thinking into chaos.

"It isn't as if I'm trying to trap a man,'' she said. "Or be underhanded. I just need help getting started. And it's perfect timing—there's a new teacher at the school. He was hired just to teach summer school, but the school board's already asked him to stay and be the coach next year. He's single and he obviously loves kids.''

Max crossed his arms over his chest. "So you're in love with the schoolteacher.''

"No, but we have a lot in common, and he seems very nice—he's already coaching the football team on his own time. And there's also the new sheriff,'' Annie said. "He hasn't been here long, and he's single, but I don't know how he feels about starting a fam-ily.''

"Hell, you've got this all thought out. What do you need me for?'' Max demanded. He didn't enjoy hear-ing about these other men, not in the slightest.

Her mouth tightened. "Because I don't know the first thing about dating, even if they did ask me out. And why would they ask? I don't know anything about clothes or looking attractive.''

"You *are* attractive.''

"Max, look at me,'' she said insistently. "Really look. Then try to tell me how great I look.''

He looked, seeing the way the setting sun turned Annie's hair into a shining cinnamon halo around her face. A faint breeze off the river blew against her shirt, outlining the slim, curving lines of her body. A pink, healthy glow brightened her face, and her eyes were defined by naturally dark lashes.

More than anything she had a mouth that begged to be kissed. Really kissed. The kind of kiss that lasted and lasted because you couldn't bear to give up the taste.

Personally Max thought any guy blind enough to miss Annie's essential beauty didn't deserve to go out with her, much less kiss her like that.

All at once he shook his head to clear it. What was he thinking? The heat must have gotten to his brains, not to mention his better judgment.

"You see what I'm talking about, don't you?" she asked. "I could try to change my image by myself, but I'm afraid I'll look ridiculous and waste a lot of time. That's why I asked for your help. And it's not like I asked you to *find* me a husband, or even introduce me to anyone. I can do that on my own."

I hope, Annie added silently.

She had flutters in her stomach, butterflies that wouldn't go away. For a couple of weeks after the doctor had delivered the bad news, she'd been numb. In shock and wanting to deny it was true. But during the past few days she'd realized she would have to take matters into her own hands. Fate obviously wasn't cooperating with biological reality.

"It's getting late," she murmured. "We should go back."

It wasn't that late, but Annie wanted to escape Max's stunned scrutiny. In hindsight she knew talking to him had been a mistake. From what she'd heard, men didn't understand a woman's desire to have a baby. And he was so antimarriage. As for the other part—not understanding her lack of feminine confidence—that was also to be expected.

Men complained that women's liberation had complicated things for them, that they didn't know how to act around a woman. But it was worse for women. Especially women raised with traditional values. Of course, it wouldn't *kill* her to ask the new schoolteacher out on a date. Rejection wasn't a fatal condition. She might even be willing to ask him out if she could do something about the way she looked.

Annie glanced down, the corners of her mouth drooping. Her jeans were too big; she knew that. And the shirt wasn't right, either. They were convenient for the kind of work she did at the store, nothing else. She'd gone into Sacramento the previous weekend, to a fancy boutique, but the saleswomen were so condescending she'd become annoyed and left without buying anything.

A pheasant suddenly burst out of the undergrowth, its wings beating noisily as it flew low to the earth. The rich colors of his feathers were bronzed by the setting sun.

The natural world had it easy, Annie decided. They didn't have to buy clothing or worry how they looked. Nature decked them out and did a glorious job of it. In some cases nature did a glorious job with humans, too.

Like with Max.

From head to toe Max Hunter was about as perfect as a man could get. A lot of men started to go soft in their thirties, but not Max. He was tall, with strong shoulders and a flat stomach—every inch of his body was balanced power and masculine grace. His face was too masculine to be beautiful, but with his high, carved cheekbones and eyes so dark they were nearly black...just looking at him made a woman breathless.

She sneaked a peek at him. He seemed very distant and far away, and she bit her lip. Their friendship was more important than getting his help.

Long rays of light lit the garden as they approached the two houses. It was on the extreme edge of Mitchellton, more out in the country than in town.

Still silent, Max walked her to the back door.

Annie put her hand on the knob, then looked back over her shoulder. "Forget what I said, Max. I'll manage by myself. I shouldn't have said anything to you about my...situation. Just knock on the door when you want to drive into Sacramento. I'll be around all day."

"What about church? Aren't you going tomorrow?"

She swallowed.

The children were putting on a special biblical play in the morning, in place of the regular service. They'd worked on the drama for weeks, but she didn't think she could get through it without crying. Right now all those sweet young faces were a reminder of everything she might never have.

"No," she said huskily. "I don't expect to attend. I've got things to do here at the house."

Max took a deep breath, wanting to say something, *anything* to fix what seemed unfixable, but Annie quickly slipped inside the house and just as quickly closed the door.

He should have said something else, he realized.

Or hugged her, the way he'd wanted to earlier. He should have found a way to comfort her. But he'd blown it, letting his ego get in the way of being a friend.

With a sigh Max returned to his grandmother's house and went out to the old sleeping porch. Grace kept a chaise lounge there, to sleep on during the occasional nights when the delta remained hot and humid. She wouldn't let him put air-conditioning in the house, saying she preferred the old swamp cooler. And in truth, on most summer days the house caught a breeze from the river, making it livable.

He lay down on the chaise and put his hands behind his head. It was monotonously quiet away from the city. No traffic or other mechanical sounds, no energy, just the call of crickets and the underlying rhythm of the river in the distance.

Max closed his eyes, but he couldn't escape the memory of Annie standing on the levee, highlighted by the sunset. And he couldn't forget the longing in her voice.

In the end his own feelings weren't important—he didn't have to share her dreams to care about them.

He would help Annie the best way he could and accept the consequences.

Chapter Three

"**H**ow did you sleep?"

The question, coming out of the pink shadows of dawn, startled Annie, and she spun around.

"Fine, Max." It was a lie, but there were certain polite lies you told to protect other people's feelings...and yourself.

He had on the same shirt and slacks he was wearing the night before, which wasn't surprising since he hadn't planned on staying over at Grace's. What *did* surprise her was seeing him at dawn, especially dawn during the summer. Max was not a morning person. While he might have changed since moving away from Mitchellton, she doubted it.

"What are you doing up in the middle of the night?" he asked.

The "middle of the night" convinced Annie that Max was just as antimorning as always.

"It's morning," she said. "You know, birds singing, sun rising, the world waking up."

"Mmm. Waking up implies you've gone to sleep."

"I see." Annie cast a swift glance at Max and saw that he was just as solemn as when she'd left him the evening before. She'd spent a few sleepless hours herself, trying to decide what she should do about Max. He was a friend, and she wanted to keep that friendship, but part of her was angry and frustrated.

Just this once, why couldn't he understand?

Wanting a baby wasn't like saying she wanted to fly to the moon. It was a goal that millions of women set every month, and she wasn't any different from them.

You should consider starting your family within the next six to nine months....

The doctor's reminder echoed in Annie's mind, reminding her that things *were* different for her. In the first place, she didn't have a husband. In the second, she wasn't the least bit experienced with men. And last, she might not be able to get pregnant if she didn't work quickly. Still, it wasn't Max's problem, and she ought to apologize.

"Annie—"

"Max—" She stopped at the same moment he did. "Go ahead," she murmured.

"No. You...go." They'd never been this awkward with each other, and she felt worse than ever. She should have realized a man would see things differently. Even more, she should have realized that Max hadn't changed.

"I'm sorry about last night," she said quickly, determined to get it out. "I shouldn't have asked you to help. I wasn't being fair."

"You just surprised me, that's all."

Surprised was an understatement, Max thought wryly. He'd never thought a great deal about Annie's romantic life. When the guys at high school were making noises about her, he'd made threats about treating her like a lady, but that was the extent of his involvement.

Annie was just...Annie.

And in less than twenty-four hours he'd had more uncomfortable thoughts about her than in all the time they'd known each other.

Well, except for that one time. Max rubbed his chin, remembering. They'd been chasing spilled change from the cash register, and her cheeks had been pink and damp from the heat. She'd seemed so breathless and elemental that he'd had a brief surge of lust before regaining his senses.

Odd, he hadn't thought about that day in years, but it still was crystal clear in his memory.

Annie leaned over and moved one of the hoses she used to water the garden. The sun was higher on the horizon, spilling more light into the yard with each passing minute, and Max groaned silently. She'd put on the shorts she used for working in the garden. They were old and stained, the cotton faded and shrunk from being laundered, and he'd seen her wearing them a hundred times...but never quite this way.

Never with his body humming with awareness.

Really, Annie had very nice long legs and a tight, sexy bottom that was just right to fill a man's hands.

Damn.

Max gritted his teeth.

"If you want, I can take you into Sacramento right

now," Annie offered as she straightened and shook drops of water from her hands.

With an effort he loosened his jaw enough to speak. "That's all right. We can wait until later."

"Aren't you worried what Miss Blakely might do to your car?"

Max shrugged. "Not really. Buffy is a spoiled brat, but she isn't stupid. She'll probably leave it at my condo or the office and express me the keys. She might even drive back to Mitchellton and look for me."

"Oh." Annie drifted deeper into the garden, and Max could almost feel it growing, embracing her as she moved within it.

Ever since he'd moved next door there had been a garden in back of the two homes. At first it was Grace's no-nonsense vegetables, with young Annie helping to tend the orderly rows of tomatoes, carrots and spinach. Now the garden spilled across both yards and was uniquely Annie's.

Riotous flowers filled every nook and cranny with a cheerful explosion of color. Trellises covered by climbing roses and wisteria sectioned areas of the yard, including a small area Annie had designed to reflect the beauty and style of a formal Japanese garden. He'd helped with that part, installing a water system that included a water lily pond and several small fountains.

"Are you *hoping* she'll come looking for you?" Annie asked after a few minutes. "Buffy, I mean."

Max frowned at the peculiar note in her voice. "No. Why?"

"She's very attractive."

"I hadn't noticed."

Annie turned and looked at him. "Really?" she asked dryly.

A grin tugged at his mouth. "Okay. I noticed it in the beginning, but the more Buffy talks, the less attractive she becomes."

"Men don't like talkative women?"

"Not when they talk like Buffy," Max said lightly, yet Annie's question had reminded him of her so-called plan. She wanted advice on catching herself a husband. Apparently even meaningless scraps of information were important to her, like a teasing remark.

He cleared his throat. "About last night—you're still planning to go manhunting, aren't you?"

Annie rolled her eyes. "I wouldn't have put it in such a crass way, but yes, I still want to find a husband. I don't have any choice, Max. If I'm going to get married and have a baby, it has to be soon."

"Then I'll help...any way I can." He could feel the fires of doom licking at his heels, but there wasn't anything else he could do. Annie was his friend, and friends looked out for each other. She could get into a lot of trouble if she wasn't careful.

"That's all right. You don't have to—"

"Yes, I do," Max said, more sharply than he'd intended. "I was wrong to get so upset when you asked. Cripes, I insisted you confide in me, then acted like a jerk when you did."

A smile hovered on her lips, and he knew she wanted to agree. He *had* acted like a jerk. A typical knee-jerk male, as his grandmother would say. Grace wasn't a man-hater by any stretch of the imagination, but she had pithy things to say about human folly.

Which raised another question…did Grace know about Annie's problem? And what would she think of the solution?

As soon as the thought formed in his mind, Max sighed. He couldn't escape the conviction that Annie was making a huge mistake and he was making an even bigger mistake getting involved.

"Annie, does my grandmother know about all of this?"

She shook her head. "I didn't want to worry her."

Max plucked a snow pea from a vine and ate the sweet, crunchy pod before answering. "Suddenly transforming yourself might make her worry even more."

Annie rinsed her feet in the water flowing from the garden hose. "Grace can take it. Besides, she's been encouraging me to make some changes, and we've talked about the sheriff and stuff. I'm sure she'll approve of anything I decide to do."

His eyebrows shot upward. If his grandmother was getting into the act, why did Annie need his help? Yet even as the thought formed, Max rejected it. Grace Hunter had been an attractive, stylish woman of her day, but she wasn't interested in modern fashion or social customs.

"What kind of changes?" he murmured.

"To start dating. She seems to think I've been turning down all the eligible men pounding down my door."

Though she said the words lightly, Max sensed a wealth of regret behind Annie's statement. Like most women, she wanted to be beautiful and desirable. And she was beautiful...she just didn't know it. Now it was worse because of her medical condition. What was it she'd said—that after surgery she probably wouldn't be able to conceive?

Somewhere, beneath all his discomfort with the idea of babies and marriage, Max began to understand Annie's uncertainty. Her identity as a woman was being threatened. It didn't matter that the ability to bear a child didn't make her any more or less of a woman, it was the way she felt.

"So," he said. "Have you changed your mind about going to church? Grandmother said there was a special program today. She's looking forward to it."

Annie shook her head. "No. But you and Grace come over for lunch after you get back."

She headed for the house, and Max took a deep breath. If only Annie could have asked him for something easy...like remodeling the house or putting in another lily pond.

He still wasn't sure how Annie thought he could help with her crazy scheme, but the whole thing was bound to have more than its share of uncomfortable moments.

"Are you sure you don't want anything from the garden?" Annie asked. "I've got tomatoes, peas, zucchini—whatever you want."

They were about to leave for Sacramento, and the hospitable side of her nature rebelled at the idea of Max going home without the truck filled with produce.

"Annie, I don't cook."

"How about some watermelon, then? You don't have to cook fruit."

He looked ready to refuse again, then nodded. "Okay. A watermelon. A small one."

Having gotten his agreement, Annie picked three large watermelons, a half dozen cantaloupes and two honeydews. Max protested, but loaded them into the back of her pickup when she insisted. He could always share with his employees, she argued, adding a basket of tomatoes and cucumbers and another of zucchini.

"We'll have to stop at my condo before going to a clothing store," Max grumbled as he fastened the tailgate. "We can't leave that stuff in the truck or someone will steal it."

Annie blinked. She knew there was more crime in the city, but it always surprised her. "They'd steal homegrown fruits and vegetables?"

"They'll take anything that isn't tied down."

"Hmm." Somehow she thought Max was exaggerating. She drove into Sacramento periodically to buy things for the store and she'd never had any problems. City life must make a person cynical, she decided. "Do you want to drive?" she asked, holding out the key. If there was one thing she *did* know about men, it was that they preferred being behind the steering wheel themselves.

Max took the key, then to her surprise, followed her to the passenger side of the ancient truck.

She frowned. "What?"

"You wanted to know how to act with a man," he muttered.

"Yes, but what—"

The question died in Annie's throat as Max gently raised her fingers from the door handle. He stood so close she felt his warmth from her shoulders to her knees.

"Yes, it's primitive," Max said in a low, rough voice. "And old-fashioned as hell. But I prefer to help a lady into the car. And out of it."

A shiver crept through Annie, despite the hot sun and Max's even hotter body. She usually avoided moments like this...moments when she couldn't ignore his overwhelming masculine appeal.

"But I don't need...that is, I get in and out of the truck all the time." Annie glanced up in time to see a rueful smile on Max's face.

"It isn't about what you need," he admitted. "It's about a man's ego—making him feel strong and protective." He lifted a strand of hair from her forehead, lightly brushing her skin in the process. "I know that, and I still can't help it."

"How do I know if some guy wants to...um, help me?"

"Body language. And giving him some time before you leap in or out."

"I see." Annie thought it was bit complicated, but she didn't protest when Max opened the truck door and tucked his hand into her elbow as she climbed inside. It seemed awkward, but she suspected it was like learning to play the piano—you got better with practice.

Max climbed in himself and adjusted the seat backward to accommodate his long legs. "How old is this truck?" he asked after a moment.

"Thirty years…next month," Annie said. "Pop got it just after my second birthday."

The motor turned over immediately, and Max whistled. "I can't imagine very many vehicles lasting that long—or sounding so good."

Annie shrugged. "I don't drive that much, and we've got a good mechanic in Mitchellton. He can keep anything running."

"What about delivering orders? You still do that at the store, don't you?"

"I do the deliveries on Saturdays. During the week one of my employees in the warehouse usually takes care of it. He prefers to use his own truck, so I pay him mileage."

"How can you deliver stuff? You can't unload hay bales or anything."

"Of course I can. It takes me a while, but I get it done."

Max mumbled something under his breath.

"What did you say?"

"Nothing."

Annie put her hands in her lap and gazed out the window, excitement bubbling in her chest. Max had suggested they visit a clothing store together, to "start" her off on her husband hunt. The malls were open, so they could chose between several department stores and boutiques.

There wasn't a saleswoman in the world who would be impervious to Max Hunter's charm. They might be condescending and irritating with her, but they'd melt with him. Nothing would be too good for Max.

It was warm, and the truck didn't have air-conditioning, so they cranked down the windows and let the delta breeze sweep around them. Annie settled back with a contented, sleepy smile. For the moment she preferred not thinking about biological deadlines or jumping into unknown territory.

She didn't mind taking care of herself, she even preferred it, but sometimes it was nice to rely on someone else, to let them take charge. Like now. She could sit and drowse and enjoy the ambiance of summer. Yet all too quickly the sounds of traffic melded with the breeze, then the scent of cars and the city, rather than the river. Then the truck stopped moving, and she wondered if they'd arrived.

"Wake up, sleepyhead," urged Max's whisky-smooth voice.

Her eyes drifted open. "I wasn't asleep."

He grinned. "Could have fooled me."

Some of Annie's contentment fled, and her forehead creased. "That was a mistake, wasn't it? I should have talked or something."

Max glanced at Annie for the hundredth time since they'd left Mitchellton. She'd swayed with each turn and bump of the road, her tempting body relaxed and trusting. "A comfortable silence is all right," he murmured.

Pushing back her hair, she yawned and stretched. "Is this your condo?"

"Yeah."

Max followed the direction of Annie's gaze as she looked around the complex. It was a far cry from Mitchellton. The landscape was groomed with meticulous care, not a blade of grass out of place. Petunias were the only flowers, and they were planted in precise rows, alternating from white to pink without a single misstep.

"It's nice."

He grinned at her polite tone. Compared to Annie's garden she probably thought the landscaping was sterile and boring, but the upscale condo was in a good location and close to his office. And it was a great investment—the value had already doubled from his original purchase price.

"And you were right about your BMW," Annie said, pointing. "There it is."

Sure enough, it was parked in front of his garage. Max looked at the car pensively. Why hadn't he noticed the "Beamer" first off? Obviously Annie's plan was beginning to short-circuit his brain.

"Do you mind if I take a quick shower and change?" he asked. "And we should take the BMW to the mall, instead of the truck."

"That's fine." Annie put out her hand to open the door, and Max deliberately cleared his throat. She jumped guiltily and waited.

"Fast learner," he said, grinning when he opened the door himself and put out a hand.

She wrinkled her nose and slid to the ground. "Don't get smug with me, Max. I still haven't forgotten about the time when you were twelve and you decided to drink a bottle of lemon extract on a dare. You were so drunk you didn't know your own name."

"Oh, God." A mixed laugh and a groan escaped his throat. "You never told Grace about that, did you?"

"Not yet."

"Brat," he mumbled, hoisting the box of melons from the back of the pickup. "I'll get that in a minute," he added when Annie reached for one of the baskets she'd put there earlier.

"I can lift a silly basket," she protested.

"No, you can open the door for me." His spare house key dangled between his fingers, and she took it with another impudent wrinkle of her nose.

Helping Annie might turn out to be fun, Max thought as she preceded him up the walkway. She was such a sweet innocent, she didn't know her own appeal. He wouldn't let her change too much, just suggest some clothes that suited her better. And he'd encourage her to take better care of herself. This business of lifting things that were too heavy and trying to do the work of two men was ridiculous.

Yeah.

It was going to work out all right.

"How about this one?" Annie held up a dress made of less fabric than one of his ties.

Max scowled.

This wasn't working out.

So far Annie had tried on ten dresses, and he'd hated each of them. They were too brief, too stark and too damned sexy. If she walked down the few streets of Mitchellton wearing something like that she'd be arrested for indecent exposure.

"Max, you haven't liked a single thing," Annie said, exasperated. She was getting frazzled with all this putting things on and taking them off. Okay, she didn't like any of the dresses, either, but she wanted to return home with at least *one* new outfit.

And the saleswomen weren't a bit of help. They were panting over Max, slinging merchandise in her direction with hardly a glance. They wouldn't know if something suited her if it hit them in the face.

The only consolation was that he didn't seem to notice them, not as women, anyway. It would have been dismal to see him cozying up to them and making a date while she was trying on stupid dresses.

"How about that shop we passed earlier?" Annie asked. "The one on the other side of the mall." She'd liked some of the garments she'd seen in the window.

"Fine by me."

Annie dropped the despised dress and grabbed her purse. If she hadn't been so tired she would have laughed at the expression on the other women's faces. Not only had they lost Max, they'd lost any potential sales.

The new store was different, not so glitzy and fashionable and the clothing seemed softer and more feminine, which was okay by Annie. She didn't think spandex and sequins were a good match for Mitchellton.

And Shelley, the sales "associate" as her badge proclaimed, was at least five months pregnant, which probably meant she wouldn't pant over a total stranger. Sure enough, the woman gave Max a pleasant smile, then focused her attention on Annie.

"May I help you?"

"Yes." Annie looked around, liking what she saw. "I need some dresses." She made a deprecating gesture toward her jeans and baggy shirt. They were clean, which was the most that could be said for them. "Actually, I need a whole new wardrobe."

Shelley gave her an appraising look, then nodded. She moved quickly around the various racks of dresses, selecting several while Annie and Max followed. "Let's make it a complete change," she said cheerily, pausing at a frothy display of underwear and bras.

Annie stopped so abruptly that Max bumped into her. Warmth burned in her cheeks at the idea of him knowing quite so much about her...clothing.

"I'm betting you're a size six," Shelley said. "And a thirty-four B, right?" A peach-colored wisp of a bra dangled from her fingers.

Annie gulped, feeling exposed, and there was a certain rigidity in Max as he stood close behind her. She fought the urge to cross her arms over her chest, and nodded. "Yes, that's right."

"Great. Let's start out with these, and see how you like them."

It was a relief to disappear into the dressing room, yet Annie couldn't keep from peeking back through the curtain at Max. He was standing with his legs apart, jaw jutted forward, as though braced for a blow. In the midst of so much feminine silk and lace, he was more out of place than the proverbial bull in a china shop.

"Don't worry," Shelley murmured, patting her shoulder. "It'll be worth it. Men hate being dragged in here, but they love the results."

"Oh, dear." Annie couldn't keep from giggling.

It had never occurred to her that Max would be embarrassed. He was *never* embarrassed. But the expression on his face was unmistakable, and for some reason it made her feel bolder.

She turned to the other woman, sensing she'd found a ally. ''Okay, let's try one of those dresses.''

''And the bra?''

Annie took the silk and lace confection. It was a world apart from practical cotton, which was probably why it appealed so much to her.

''Why not?'' she agreed.

Chapter Four

"**I** knew that would look great on you," Shelley, the sales associate, declared from behind the curtain.

"It does look nice, but doesn't it seem a little..." Annie's voice trailed. She said something softly that Max was apparently not intended to hear, and a burst of laughter followed.

Max grimaced, then grinned despite his discomfort in the utterly feminine shop. From the amount of laughing and chatter going on the dressing room he could tell that Annie and the saleswoman were hitting it off.

He was glad, because he'd detected a faint shadow in Annie's face when she'd seen the other woman's swollen stomach, and his own stomach had knotted when he'd heard her unconscious sigh. He wasn't good with emotional stuff; it reminded him of his mother and father's screeching fights, both with each other, and with their subsequent spouses.

Only…the comparison wasn't fair to Annie. She was a do-gooding sweetheart, while his parents were sticks of emotional dynamite. When Annie got upset it was mostly over important stuff. He hunched his shoulders, uncomfortable all over again because the important stuff to Annie was getting married and having a kid.

"What do you think, Max?"

He looked up and blinked as Annie stepped around the dressing room curtain.

"Isn't it perfect?" She spread her arms and twirled, plainly comfortable in the dress, though it was a far cry from her usual jeans and shirts. Made of a soft, flowing material, it clung to her curves without deliberately drawing attention to them.

Somehow that made it worse.

This was a dress that challenged a man—seemingly demure, with little pearl buttons running its full length. The sweetheart neck dropped low enough to reveal the first swell of her breasts. On top of everything else, the fabric was practically transparent with the light from the dressing room shining behind her. He could see the outline of sleek thighs…even the suggestion of lacy underwear.

A definite challenge.

The kind that made a man think about the ways he could get the dress off, including struggling with all those silly buttons, button by delicious button. He didn't *want* a man thinking that way about Annie. She was too naive and innocent to protect herself, so he had to do it for her.

"You need a slip," he muttered.

"Oh."

The disappointment in Annie's eyes made Max wince. He was supposed to be helping, but what he wanted was to cover her with a flour sack and drag her back to Mitchellton. Nice, safe, boring Mitchellton. Now that he thought about it, there were some advantages to small towns that didn't change.

"Shelley, Max says I need a slip. What kind should I get?" Annie asked the sales associate.

"*Max* is wrong," the other woman said, glaring at Max. "And it wouldn't work right with such a full skirt and that slit up the front."

Slit?

Max began to sweat in earnest as Annie spread the skirt and examined the opening in question. Sure enough, the tiny buttons were unfastened up to mid-thigh, and Annie certainly didn't seem shy about showing him all those exposed inches. He didn't have the slightest clue why this dress bothered him even more than the outrageously provocative outfits she'd tried on earlier, but it did.

"So button the rest of the buttons," he growled.

"It's meant to be that way," Shelley said, giving him another fierce look. Another time he might have been taken aback since he was accustomed to women liking him, but right now he was too flumoxed to do anything but stare at the peach-toned skin of Annie's legs. The dress, which at first glance appeared modest and old fashioned, was anything *but*.

"It might be better to fasten a few more," he said, willing to compromise. "The slit goes pretty high. Remember how conservative Mitchellton is about that sort of stuff."

A stubborn expression crossed Annie's face. "It's less revealing than a pair of shorts."

"That's different."

"Not really." Annie turned and gazed at herself in a nearby mirror. She liked the reflection looking back at her, the woman revealed in the oh-so-feminine dress. So why didn't Max like it on her?

She wanted to kick him.

There was nothing wrong with the skirt. The gowns she'd tried on at the other stores were much more revealing, better suited to actresses and fashion models than a normal person leading a normal life.

This was pretty and felt right. Still...Annie chewed her lip, trying to sort out her irritation with Max's comments and her priorities.

Okay. Max didn't like it, and he was the expert. That's why she'd asked him to help her, so she wouldn't waste time with things men didn't appreciate. That was the worst part about this whole thing, she didn't have a second to waste making mistakes.

"I guess I'd better try something else," she murmured, giving the skirt a last, longing stroke.

"*No.*"

The loud exclamation made both her and Shelley jump, and they both looked at him in surprise. "What?"

"Go ahead. It's not that bad," he muttered. "I mean, it looks pretty nice."

"But if you don't like—"

"I like it fine." Max sounded ready to chew nails, which Annie could understand. He hadn't expected to spend his Sunday afternoon doing something so boring as picking out dresses for her to wear.

"Okay," Shelley said briskly. "That's one dress toward your new wardrobe. Now, let's try something with a little more color."

Annie's spirits rose again, and she decided that as long as Max was willing to help her, he could be as grumpy as he wanted. He was entitled. She impulsively flew over and gave him a kiss on the cheek.

"Thanks for doing this, Max. You're wonderful."

Max slumped against the wall as Annie rushed back into the dressing area. Shelley lingered, long enough to give him a cool, head-to-toe examination. It was the kind of examination a scientist gave bacteria under a microscope...which was the size he felt after being churlish over the dress. "Try being a little more wonderful, Max," the woman drawled. "Okay?"

Lord, would this nightmare ever end?

"Shelley," Annie called. "Do you have any front-clasp bras? I've always wanted to try one."

Max groaned. Front-clasp bras? The kind that gave easy access to a lover?

Apparently, the nightmare was only just starting.

Annie hummed to herself as they drove back to Max's condo. While she didn't have the kind of new wardrobe a socialite like Buffy Blakely would consider adequate, she did have an astonishing assortment of new clothing, including two voile nightgowns that were so sheer they were practically indecent. And she had new underwear, too—pretty, sexy underwear that wasn't the least bit practical.

Then Max had tried to pay for everything, saying something about it being an apology. Not that she'd let him buy her clothing. It was enough that he was advising her on the romance thing.

Barely saying a word, he helped transfer her packages from the trunk of the BMW to the truck.

"Thanks, Max. I'll never be able to repay you," she said.

"You don't owe me anything," he replied brusquely. "Look, I'll come out next Saturday night and we'll have that practice date you talked about."

"It's all right," she said hastily. "You don't have to do that."

"I want to. Did I say I didn't want to?"

Annie hung on to her temper. What was wrong with her these days? Normally she was the calmest, most even-tempered person around. It certainly wasn't as if she were pregnant already and could blame her emotions on rampaging hormones.

"Please, Max," she said with barely an edge in her voice. "You're really busy, and I've taken enough of your time. I'm just trying to be considerate."

"I didn't ask you to be considerate, I said I'd help you with this crazy plan of yours, and that's what I'm going to do."

"It isn't crazy!"

"It is, too," he shouted back.

Hurt and anger struggled for supremacy in Annie's chest, though it wasn't as if she didn't understand. Marriage was Max's biggest hang-up. She couldn't expect him to change his mind just because he was helping her, and obviously he hadn't.

A neighbor stuck his head out of his open garage and watched them curiously.

Swell.

Max hated scenes of any kind, and he'd probably blame her for causing this one. Well, it wasn't her fault. Annie lifted her chin and returned the stranger's stare until he disappeared again.

All at once Max's face cleared and he rocked forward on the balls of his feet. "Sorry," he murmured, touching her cheek. "I'm an unreasonable jerk."

Annie swallowed. It was hard thinking about anything when Max had that warm look in his eyes. Of course, it had fooled her before, back when they were teenagers. Maybe if he'd kissed her all those years ago it would have cured her of being so susceptible now. Sort of like having a flu shot...it didn't protect you 100 percent, but it helped.

"So, do we have a date?" he coaxed.

"Okay," she agreed slowly. "But you aren't a jerk."

"Still arguing with me, huh?"

She studied him carefully, noting his involuntary frown, despite the teasing note in his voice. "Mmm, that's right, I remember," she said lightly. "You don't like women who argue. Do all men feel the same way, or is it just you?"

He pulled away a few inches—inches she desperately needed to breath. What was it about becoming more aware of herself as a woman, that made her even more aware of Max as a man?

Heck, she didn't *want* to be aware of Max. The last thing she needed was to be confused about her goals.

"It was just a joke," he said.

"But you really *don't*—" His hand over her mouth smothered the protest and she stared at him.

"Forget it, Annie. I'll see you on Saturday. Is seven all right?"

She nodded, unable to say anything through Max's fingers. He moved slightly, and she could almost imagine his thumb was caressing her lower lip before he dropped his arm, releasing her. A hollow, achy feeling went through her body.

Annie sidled past him, shaking and willing to do anything as long as she could get away. *Fast.*

"Saturday at seven is fine," she murmured. "I'll see you then."

Still quiet, he put his fingers on her elbow, helping her into the cab. She'd nearly forgotten about that part again and felt more awkward than ever about the small male-female ritual. Max shut the door, slapped his hands lightly on the side, then stepped away.

Annie clumsily put the truck into gear and sent it lurching and jolting down the first few feet of the street. She was too shaken to care. Her mouth still tingled from its contact with Max's hand, and the quivering in her tummy kept getting worse, rather than better.

"I'm an idiot," she muttered once she'd gotten out of the city. She pulled off the road and stopped the truck, glaring at the dust adorning the dashboard.

Asking Max for romantic guidance must have been the biggest lamebrain idea in the world—certainly the worst idea *she'd* ever had. He had the kind of sex appeal that made other men seem pale by comparison.

How was she supposed to fall in love with someone else with Max standing around? It was like asking a child to choose between chocolate and a nice, healthy serving of broccoli for dinner. The broccoli was hands down the wisest choice—the only right choice—but the chocolate tasted better.

All at once Annie threw back her head and laughed. "There you go, overreacting again," she announced.

Her father had always said she was a dramatic child, so at least it was nothing new. Max was only going to be around for the *beginning* of her plan. The lesson stage. He'd get her started, and then she'd be on her own. He wouldn't be "standing around" anywhere, especially where other men were concerned.

Besides, there was a world of difference between love and friendship and lust. She was *friends* with Max. That's all. Falling in love with another man would cure any stray feelings of lust.

Right.

Nodding her head decisively, Annie pulled out onto the road again. She could still make this thing work.

On Saturday, at precisely 6:57 in the evening, Annie surveyed herself in the mirror and grinned with delight. She'd never looked better.

The past week had been more fun than she could ever remember having. On Monday she'd worn one of her new outfits—a pair of close-fitting jeans and a camisole top with spaghetti straps that exposed her shoulders. Darnell and one of his teenage friends had actually whistled before recognizing her in the parking lot.

Then on Tuesday old Morris Jeppers had driven his car off the road because he was distracted watching her walk to the post office. His wife had laughed and told Annie all about it when she'd rushed over to see if they were okay. Morris's face had turned the shade of a ripe tomato, so Annie had smiled and sincerely thanked him for noticing.

The rest of the week had gone by with similar reactions from other employees and customers. She hadn't seen the sheriff or the new high school teacher yet, but she would probably see them at church on Sunday. Now the only thing she had to worry about was getting through a date with Max.

"Not a real date," she murmured, smoothing the tip of her finger over her eyebrow. "Just something for practice."

The doorbell rang, and Annie started guiltily. She hurried down the stairs, as much as her new high heels would allow, and threw open the door.

"Max," she said breathlessly. "I'm sorry. I meant to be outside waiting so you wouldn't have to get out of the car."

Max looked at Annie and felt as if he'd been punched in the gut. Her midnight-blue gown was subtly sophisticated, with a complicated crisscrossing of thin velvet straps across her shoulders and above her breasts. The blue enhanced the color of her eyes and made her skin gleam with the translucent beauty of a pearl.

"I really am sorry," she repeated, and Max shook his head.

"Nonsense," he said hoarsely.

"But I should have been out—"

"No." He pulled himself together with an effort. "First lesson in dating—expect your escort to come to the door for you."

A confused frown pursed her mouth. "That seems rude. Why shouldn't I be considerate?"

"Because you don't want your date to think you're too eager."

"But what if I *am* eager? What's wrong with letting a man know that? It seems much more straightforward than playing a game."

Max wasn't in any mood to explain the peculiar workings of the male mind, about pursuit and winning, or about the admittedly primeval instincts that continued to drive his sex. To be honest—if only to himself—he didn't want Annie to get good at the games between men and women.

"It's just the way things are," he growled. "Okay?"

"Okay." Some of the enthusiasm faded from Annie's face, and Max sighed.

"Look, I admit it. A lot of social customs are stupid. Positively primitive," he said, throwing up his hands in a gesture of defeat.

Teaching Annie was turning out to be even more educational for him. No wonder she was confused by some of the rituals between men and women. Seen through an innocent's eyes, some of them *were* ridiculous.

"Oh...how pretty." Annie gestured to the bouquet waving in front of her face. "You better take those over to Grace before we leave."

Max had forgotten the bunch of flowers he'd been holding behind his back, and he stared at the roses for a stupid moment. This evening was *not* going the way he'd planned. He was accustomed to being more polished and sophisticated than this—not the sort of guy who forgets he brought flowers for a girl and forgets to give them to her...to the point where she has to prompt the gift.

Except...he looked at Annie and realized she didn't have the least notion he'd brought the roses for her. She truly thought they were for his grandmother.

"They're for you," he said more calmly.

"Oh." A pleased pink brightened her cheeks, and she took the bouquet as if it were a bunch of diamonds. "I've never gotten flowers before. I'll put them in some water."

Annie turned and hurried to the kitchen, at the same time reminding herself that Max had only brought flowers as part of her lesson on dating.

There was only one suitable vase in the house, and even though she knew Max's gift didn't mean anything special, Annie smiled as she arranged the blossoms in a piece of her mother's Limoges porcelain. Once, a long time ago, she used to dream about putting a boyfriend's flowers in her mother's special vase. She stroked the velvety petals of the roses, then leaned down to inhale their sweet fragrance.

What was it about roses that was so romantic?

"I just realized I forgot to tell you something," Max said, startling her.

Annie looked up. "Yes?"

"You look beautiful."

"Uh...thank you," Annie said faintly.

At least that was something she hadn't been mistaken about—the admiration she'd seen in his dark eyes when she first opened the front door. Still, Max might be complimenting her because it was expected—part of those social customs he obviously didn't like to explain.

Annie clung to her smile with an effort. She had to remember this wasn't a real date, it was for practice; a prelude to the real thing. But it was hard not to wish that Max really cared, that he wanted something more than the casual friendship they'd always shared.

Idiot.

Yeah, she was an idiot. Max wasn't about to see her in a new light after all these years. Why would he? He was so gorgeous he probably had every eligible bachelorette in Sacramento beating a path to his door.

Yet she wondered, did those eager women see what she saw? When they looked, did they just see the handsome face, or did they recognize the strength in his arms and shoulders and legs, the humor in his eyes, tinged with a kind of bleak loneliness that never seemed to leave? Max was strong and quick and knew how to laugh, but he was also the most solitary person she knew.

"Are you ready?" he asked.

"Yes, all done," she said, dropping her hands away from the roses. "Sorry to keep you waiting."

Max frowned. He hated her polite tone—almost as much as he missed the breathless surprise his compliment had brought to her face. In the space of a five seconds, without a single word, she'd switched from being the sweet Annie he'd always known, to being a stranger.

"You didn't keep me waiting. But it's probably going to get cool this evening. Shouldn't you bring a sweater or something?"

"I'll be fine."

He could always loan her his jacket or something, Max decided. Outside she pulled the door of the house shut—without locking it, he noticed—and walked ahead of him to the BMW, her hips swaying gently. She was wearing strappy new sandals with heels, so he guessed she'd gone shopping again.

Good.

He nodded, trying to be glad. Annie was taking the initiative, not waiting to ask his advice on everything. She was even wearing a touch of makeup—just enough to darken her lashes and make her lips glossy. With her delicate complexion she didn't need to plaster her face with a lot of artificial color.

"I was thinking…maybe you should lock the house," he muttered, trying not to think about how nice her mouth looked with that shiny stuff on it.

"We never lock in Mitchellton."

It was that small-town mentality, the sense of being safe. But he knew crime occurred in small towns as well as cities, and Max's jaw tightened. "I want that door locked," he insisted. "And I want you to promise that you'll always lock when you leave, and also at night."

"But—"

"No buts. Promise, Annie." He could see the astonishment in her eyes, but it didn't matter. This was part of making her take better care of herself. He'd gotten his grandmother to agree she'd lock the house, especially at night, now he'd get the same promise from Annie.

"All right. But I'll need to have a key made first…I haven't had one for years. Lost it somewhere." She made a vague gesture with her hand and shrugged.

Naturally. Max noisily let out a breath. "I'll come over tomorrow and put new locks on the doors. And I'll check the windows, too," he added.

"I can take care of it, Max."

"So can I."

"Honestly, you act like I'm a helpless two-year-old," Annie said, exasperated. "I can take care of my own locks. And my windows for that matter. I've been taking care of myself for years, you know."

"Didn't say you couldn't."

Max opened the passenger door of the beamer and held out his hand. With the haughty dignity of a grand duchess, Annie touch her fingers to his and slid into the car. A good portion of her leg was exposed before she settled the skirt over her knees, and Max gritted his teeth. She'd gone from baggy jeans to sheer silk hosiery in less than a week. He didn't know why he'd never noticed she had legs that wouldn't quit. Now it seemed to be the only thing he noticed.

Oh, yeah, and what about her bustline? Like you haven't noticed that part of her anatomy? The part cupped by a strapless bra?

A choking sensation rose in Max's chest and he gritted his teeth as he dropped behind the wheel. Annie was off-limits. He was just doing this date thing with her so she would get some pointers on going out with other men. It certainly wasn't a real date with any sexual nuances.

"Are you all right?" Annie asked.

"Fine. Why?"

"You seem a little...stressed."

Stressed didn't begin to describe the way he felt,

but Max made a conscious effort to relax. "It's been a long week."

"Hmm." He sensed Annie's eyes watching him, then she sighed. "I could fix us some dinner at the house."

"You cooked last time. Besides, this is a date."

"Practice date," she reminded him, which was really annoying. For Pete's sake, he knew it was a practice date. Annie was practicing her feminine skills on him so she could go out and catch herself a husband.

"Yeah. Right. Practice," he mumbled.

The expression on Max's face made Annie want to laugh, yet it also made her sad. She'd confided things to Max that she'd never told anyone else. After everything was said and done, could they go back to just being friends? The same old *comfortable* friends as long as she ignored his killer sex appeal? She supposed it was up to him.

"Hey, do you still like Italian?" Max asked, sounding more normal.

"Love it."

"Great." He drove out of the yard. "There's a restaurant in Old Sacramento that will make you think you've died and gone to heaven."

Annie let out a long breath and stroked the thin velvet fabric over her lap. She felt so strange, and it wasn't just the new clothing or the unfamiliar garters holding her stockings in place. It was a totally feminine feeling—strange and wonderful and frightening, all at the same time.

Chapter Five

"**W**hat do you think?"

Annie savored the last bite of her tiramisu, a richly flavored concoction of whipped cream, liqueur and cake. "You're right, I'm in heaven."

Max's answering smile was tinged with strain. He'd never realized Annie was so sensual. She enjoyed her food without any self-consciousness...and the way she licked her fork was practically indecent.

"Maybe I'll try making tiramisu for the ice-cream social on Sunday," she said.

"Won't that be a problem at church with the liqueur in it?" he muttered.

"Mmm, no. The preacher's wife makes a rum cake that could knock you out of your socks."

"A little...pungent?"

Annie laughed. "Something like that. We have to be careful not to light any candles near our plates for fear of serving it flambé."

"And the church along with it?"

"Right. The school board has discreetly requested she make something else to donate to the carnival bake sale. They didn't think a 100-proof cake would look good at a school fund-raiser."

"Grandmother mentioned that the carnival has gotten better. I remember it used to be pretty hokey."

She sent him a glance from under her lashes. "It's still hokey, that's why we love it. Small-town heaven."

"Mmm, yes." Max didn't want to get into an argument about small towns. His feelings had always been mixed on that subject; certainly enough to make him want to leave as soon as he was old enough to be legally an adult.

"I always got assigned to stuffing hot dog buns and slinging relish, but I always wished I could have worked in the kissing booth," Annie murmured, her face wistful.

"No, you didn't."

A small frown turned her lips into a perfect pout, and Max's own lips twitched. Annie didn't pout, she went straight to the heart of anything she cared about—pouting just wasted time.

"I know what I wanted," she said. "Not that anyone would have wanted to kiss me, but it would have been fun."

Yeah, well, Max had spent plenty of time at the kissing booth when he was in high school, usually for free. And it *had* been fun, especially for a teenager with overeager hormones and an itch to explore the pneumatic curves beneath a cheerleader's sweater.

Like it or not, Annie simply hadn't been that sort of girl then, any more than she was now.

"Stuffing hot dog buns wasn't such a bad job," he mumbled. "And you looked cute in the apron."

Annie rolled her eyes. "It was a butcher's apron and covered me from my neck to my knees. I felt like a mummy wrapped up in that thing—not that you'd know, you never once came by the hot dog stand. We weren't exactly your speed."

Max looked at Annie curiously. He hadn't known she'd wanted to volunteer at the carnival kissing booth. She'd always been just Annie, working wherever she was needed. Odd, they'd lived next door to each other, but their lives were so different, even then. Until recently he hadn't thought about the things she'd missed.

"I think the boys would have lined up to kiss you," he said quietly. "Right around the block. You've got a great mouth." *Too* great, he added silently. It could make a man do things he'd regret the next day.

A startled pleasure filled Annie's blue eyes. "Th-thank you."

"Tell you what...we'll go to the carnival together this year. I'm sure the schoolteacher will be attending."

"Oh, yes. He's been really active helping to organize everything."

"Well then, it'll give you a chance to see him without looking too obvious."

"Okay." She swiped a fleck of whipped cream from her plate and delicately licked it from the tip of her finger. The air hissed from Max's lungs, and the heat in the restaurant went up at least a hundred degrees. The man sitting at a nearby table stared transfixed, along with the waiter who had flirted with Annie all evening. Max gave them a hard look until they noticed, and hastily shifted their attention.

"Here...have mine," he said, shoving his untouched plate in her direction.

"Don't you want it?"

"No. I'm full. I had the prime rib, remember?" *Besides, I'd rather watch you eat it.*

Annie lifted a curl of shaved chocolate from the offered plate and dropped it into her mouth. "Yum. I usually don't bother with dessert at home. This is wonderful."

She ate his tiramisu with the same pleasure she'd consumed her own. Finally she sat back in her chair and touched her fingers to her tummy. Though Max knew the gesture simply meant "I'm full," it only served to draw attention to the slender lines of her body.

Annie sighed. "Now I feel totally decadent. Thank you."

"My pleasure." Yet even as he said the words, Max squirmed. He wasn't supposed to be having any sort of response to Annie, much less a response that didn't have any place in friendship. He'd known Annie most of his life, and he thought she was terrific...just not the kind of terrific that led to satin sheets and candlelight.

It had to be the dress. Somehow Annie had found a dress that bridged the gap between her innocence and the sophisticated fashions of the day. She looked perfect. Entirely too perfect for his comfort.

"Do you eat here often?" Annie asked.

"What?" Max shook himself. "Sometimes. Uh, you, uh, didn't get that outfit last Sunday. You must have gone shopping again." The comment sounded banal, even to his ears, but his usual intelligence was short-circuiting at the moment.

"Yes." Annie sipped her coffee. "I realize it might be a little too dressy," she murmured, looking down at the soft velvet fabric. "But I couldn't resist. And I figured your taste ran to more elegant restaurants than the ones around Mitchellton, so talked myself into it."

"Don't you think your schoolteacher or the sheriff will take you to a nice place?"

A faint pink stained her cheeks. "That isn't what I meant. Besides, they aren't *mine* yet, and I only want one of them. I mean, I want one of them to…and me, too." She stopped, flustered.

He leaned forward. "Yes?"

"I want to fall in love," Annie said quietly. "And to be loved right back. I told you that."

"Right."

Annie didn't understand the restless tension in Max as he watched her. So far they'd had a lovely evening, and apparently she hadn't said or done anything too wrong, because Max hadn't mentioned any errors on her part.

The waiter put the check on the table, pausing to give her a warm smile. "Did you enjoy the cake, miss?"

Before she could answer, Max tossed a credit card down. "Here," he barked, dragging the man's attention away.

"Yes, sir."

"Heavens, Max. You're acting like a bear with a sore paw," Annie scolded when they were alone again. "If you didn't feel like going out tonight you should have let me cook dinner. I *did* offer."

Max gave her a dark, brooding glance. "I just don't like the way that guy looks at you."

"He's being nice, that's all."

"I don't call it nice when someone practically drools all over every course and can't take his eyes off your date."

Her eyes widened in astonishment. If it had been any other man but Max, she might have wondered if he was jealous. But this wasn't any other man, it was Max, and Max would never be jealous in a hundred years. Not over her.

All at once she chuckled. "Oh, I understand. Do guys get jealous over waiters very often?"

It took Max several seconds to realize Annie thought his behavior was another "dating" lesson, and he didn't know whether he should be relieved or frustrated with her innocence.

"Occasionally," he said.

"How should I handle it?"

His mind blanked, mostly because this was the first time he'd ever gotten uptight about a waiter showing too much attention to his date. Not that he was jealous...*much*. He just didn't think Annie knew how to deal with that type of attention, and he wanted to be sure she was okay.

A jab from his conscience made him wince, but he ignored the twinge along with the uncomfortable knowledge that he was behaving irrationally over a woman he'd known since he was eleven years old.

"Uh, well..." Max stopped and cleared his throat.

A mischievous expression flitted across Annie's face, then she leaned forward with a sincere smile. She stroked her forefinger across his wrist and down the back of his hand.

"I'm sorry, Max," she purred in a low voice. "I really didn't notice him acting any special way. Don't be angry." Then she spoiled the sexy effect by wrinkling her nose. "Jeez, that sounded dumb. I guess I'd better practice."

Max looked at her finger, still stroking a lazy circle across his skin, and realized she hadn't spoiled anything. As though an invisible net was being drawn over his body, he felt her touch clear to his toes. If she did that to her sheriff or schoolteacher they'd drag her out of the restaurant and into the closest bed. He must have been blind not to see how desirable she was with that sexy little body and sweet smile.

"You did fine," he muttered.

Max kept a tight rein on his emotions when the credit slip was returned for signature by the same smiling waiter. This was a restaurant he enjoyed, and he wouldn't want to be banned for starting a brawl with one of its employees.

"It's been a long time since I've been down in Old Sacramento. Would you mind taking a walk?" Annie asked as they stepped outside.

"Sounds fine." Max drew her hand into the crook of his arm as they walked down the board sidewalk. The sun was down, and only a small amount of light remained in the western sky, but there were old-fashioned streetlamps spaced along the street and strings of white twinkle lights shining in various courtyards.

"I don't get it…if a woman goes out with you, it must mean she likes you, so why does it matter if someone else pays attention to her?" Annie asked as they stepped out on the brick-paved street that faced the waterfront. The slightly uneven surface made navigating in her brand-new high heels even more tricky, and she kept her eyes focused on the ground.

"Men are territorial," Max admitted. "But it isn't just us men. Women get jealous, too."

Women get jealous, too.

Annie thought about it and realized she'd want to slap any cute waitress who salivated over Max. She sure hadn't liked it when the women at the clothing shops had flirted with him, though she could hardly blame them. There was something so very exciting about his dark good looks and tall strength.

Of course, she didn't have any right to get jealous over Max, and it wasn't as if he was planning to get married to anyone. He was the original lone bachelor, dedicated to his unmarried state. They could be friends forever without him having a wife to get upset about it.

Distracted by her thoughts, Annie's heel caught on the rough edge of a brick and she stumbled. Before she could even think of catching herself, Max caught her close.

Annie swallowed.

This was the perfect kissing situation, but she couldn't begin to think, not with her body pressed to his from her breast to her knees. And his hands…one of them was cupping her bottom and doing wicked things to her thought process, while the other had hold of her rib cage, just below the curve of her breast.

It seemed like hours they stood locked together, staring at each other, before Max mumbled something unintelligible and released her.

"That—uh, thanks," she said.

"Are you okay?"

"Me? Oh, sure." Her laugh was forced.

How could she be okay when her heart was racing a mile a minute and her muscles were refusing to cooperate? She didn't know how to handle feelings that strong. Sexual curiosity had always been softer for her, more of a floating, shimmery sort of sensation. Not like this. Not like free-falling from an airplane.

Max was definitely the last man she should ever be involved with. She didn't want something that tore her apart, she wanted love and tenderness and fidelity—not wild explosions and the ground shifting beneath her feet.

Annie carefully stepped backward. She wanted to avoid any repeats of being grabbed close and getting confused again. Max was an exciting guy, but he was hardly husband material.

"That was klutzy of me," she said.

"No. It's the street. And those shoes," Max added. "You're not used to heels, are you?"

He knew perfectly well she wasn't accustomed to heels, and she scowled. "Leave my shoes out of this." It wasn't fair since the shoes *were* responsible for tripping her, but she wasn't in the mood to be fair.

Max's expression became less unreadable and a lot

more confused. "Annie, is something bothering you?"

"No."

It was a bald-faced lie, but she couldn't explain, it would be too embarrassing. She couldn't confess her attraction to him, he'd either laugh his head off or run for the hills.

Anyway, attraction wasn't the same as love. Attraction was a chemical reaction caused by hormones. Love lasted. Chemical reactions burned themselves out.

Unsettled, Annie turned and saw the *Delta King* at the dock, an old riverboat that had been converted into a hotel. She'd always dreamed of a honeymoon spent traveling up and down the Mississippi River on an old stern-wheeler, so seeing the *Delta King* should have made her feel better.

But it didn't. She was all mixed up when it came to Max, feeling like a kid with her first crush. Except she was a little old for a crush, not to mention being more than a little embarrassed by the whole thing.

"Annie?" Max's hands settled on her shoulders, and she shivered, despite the warmth in his hard palms. "You seem awfully quiet all of a sudden."

"I was thinking."

"About what?"

His breath lifted the hair at her temple, and she sighed. In all honesty Max terrified her—the way he made her feel, the intense emotions in his eyes that she didn't always understand. It was more than him being such a complicated man, it was the way he lived his life, practically attacking the process of living. No sitting still for Max, he charged ahead with the speed and power of a jet engine.

Her life was more like the Sacramento River on a lazy summer afternoon. Small pleasures and passions were her speed, things like petting the cat or impulsively running through a sprinkler set out on the lawn.

"Annie?" Max repeated, pulling her more closely against his chest.

She shivered again and tried to think of something that would put some distance between them, both physically and emotionally. Nearby the lights of the steamboat beckoned through the growing night, and she got an idea.

"Have you ever stayed at the *Delta King?* I understand the captain's cabin is wonderful."

"Never been there," Max said, his voice rumbling through her. "When I was living in Boston, I stayed with Grandmother whenever I visited California."

"Well, if I can't spend my honeymoon on the Mississippi, I hope we can stay for a week on the *Delta King*. It seems awfully romantic, even if it doesn't travel up and down the river any longer."

As she expected, Max stiffened. In some ways he was really predictable: anything to do with weddings and marriage was guaranteed to put a board up his back. "Honeymoon?"

"You know, a honeymoon. The part that follows 'I do,'" Annie said lightly. "Where the bride and groom go after the reception?"

"I know what honeymoons are," he said through clenched teeth. "My parents live from honeymoon to honeymoon. It's getting late, I'll take you home."

Annie barely kept from smiling as they walked

back to Max's car. She might be out of her depth with Max as a woman, but she wasn't doing too badly on the friend front.

Humming softly as they drove back to Mitchellton, she thought about the next step in her practice date. The next step being a good-night kiss. Would Max do anything about it, or would he assume she knew that part? If anything, it was the part she knew the least about.

When they reached the porch Annie drew a breath for courage. He seemed ready to leave, so she put a hand on his arm to stop him.

"I just wondered…what should I do about good-night kisses?" she asked.

"*What?*"

Annie frowned. Honestly, Max kept forgetting he was teaching her about the ins and outs of dating. He plainly didn't see her in a romantic sense, even in connection with another man. The confidence she'd gained over the past week wavered slightly, then she decided it was perfectly annoying, and Max didn't have any business thinking of her in such an asexual way. Heck, she saw *him* as a man, though it wasn't entirely comfortable.

"A good-night kiss," she repeated. "How soon is it all right to kiss your date? I mean, isn't there still a double standard about a woman being 'fast' if she kisses on a first date, but a guy is just lucky?"

Max leaned against a support post of the porch and groaned silently. The whole thing was so frustrating, yet underneath he admired Annie's determination. She'd decided to change her life and was going about it with a vengeance. He didn't have the heart to tell her that the modern double standard no longer re- volved around an innocent kiss, but around having sex on the first date. And even that wasn't necessarily considered "fast."

"Don't think so much about it," he advised. "A first kiss isn't such a big deal anymore."

"But what should I do? I figure the sheriff and the coach are pretty different, so they'd approach it dif- ferently. How should I act?"

The thought of Annie kissing another man was more than Max could stand. He'd seen half the male restaurant patrons watch her with sex on their minds, listened to her talk about weddings and honeymoons, and now he was faced with her deciding when she should kiss two specific men. And *how* she should kiss them. He didn't know either the coach or sheriff, and it wasn't logical, but at the moment he hated both of them.

"Let it be spontaneous," Max said brusquely. "Stop overanalyzing everything."

"Oh. Like this, you mean?" An impish smile curved Annie's mouth. She threw her arms around his neck and gave him a quick kiss on the lips.

As kisses went, it was one of the most innocent he'd ever received, but it hiked up Max's temperature more than he'd thought possible. If Annie went around kissing men like that she'd end up in real trou- ble.

Annie drew back. "Was that okay, Max?"

Telling himself he was just teaching her a lesson, he cupped the soft line of her jaw and brushed the ball of his thumb across her lips. They weren't shiny any longer, instead they felt like warm satin.

"Uh, Max?"

"Shhh."

The night was cool, moist, filled with the scent of the garden and the nearby river. And of Annie. She smelled like spring flowers and something mysterious and essentially feminine. He must have been blind for all these years not to really see her.

Annie was more than just the girl next door. More than his friend with a heart of gold. She was a woman—more innocent than most, but in a world of jaded experience, innocence was far more intriguing than an experienced swing of the hips and a come-hither smile.

He wanted to kiss her, *really* kiss her, and it scared the living daylights out of him. Max couldn't remember the last time he'd been so urgent about kissing a woman.

Worry about it later, screamed his body.

That was right, he could worry about things later...sort it out in the quiet privacy of his condominium. Right now he should teach Annie about being careful with men and kissing them so impulsively.

Shaken by the need clawing at him, Max concentrated on something small, something he could manage. He lifted both of Annie's hands and kissed each palm in turn, at the last flicking his tongue against the sensitive center. He sensed, more than felt, her jump of surprise.

"You have nice hands," he whispered.

"They, uh, aren't very soft. I'm sure Buffy has much nicer ones."

"Yours are better," Max said sincerely.

He liked the feel of Annie's skin, partly because

she *didn't* have the pampered hands of a society deb. There were small calluses on her fingers, and her nails were cut short—exactly what you'd expect with someone who worked so hard. But they were still soft and gentle in comparison with his own large hands, still open and generous.

Guilt ate the edges of Max's conscience. He wanted to be just as generous as Annie, to help her find what she wanted in a husband, but he didn't feel that way. The selfish truth was, he wanted things to remain the same, the way they'd always been.

Pushing the thought away, Max kissed his way up the inside of Annie's wrist, tasting her, counting the rapid beat of her heart with his lips, sucking at the point where her pulse throbbed the hardest. He could tell she was shocked by the small intimacy, then an instant later her body relaxed, and she let out a long breath.

"That's it, baby," he encouraged. There were a thousand lines he could give her, the kind men threw off to seduce women, but he couldn't think of one.

In the dark it was easy to forget Annie was the girl who'd seen him stinking drunk from downing a whole bottle of lemon extract, or the teenager who'd turned the garden hose on him for eating the pie she'd made to enter in the county fair cooking contest. Damn, that had been a good pie. Worth the impromptu shower.

Don't think, advised his baser instincts. If he thought too much he might remember some of the things he didn't want to remember…like his principles.

Max tugged at Annie's hip until she leaned full into him. The thin velvet of her dress did little to disguise the round imprint of her breasts against his chest. That, along with the hardened points of her nipples, was sufficient to banish any lingering moral questions.

"It's chilly out tonight," he muttered, moving her slowly back and forth against him, thoroughly enjoying those tight feminine peaks, though he wasn't responsible for their condition. It might be summer, but nights on the delta could be downright cold, and a woman's body reacted to the cold. It didn't mean she was aroused. He wasn't even sure that he wanted Annie to be aroused, just warned.

"I-is it?"

"What?" he asked, forgetting he'd said anything.

"Cold?"

"Yeah."

Annie was enough shorter that Max decided he wanted her a little closer to his level, so he put both hands around her waist and lifted her to the wide porch railing.

That was better.

The velvet of Annie's skirt whispered against her silk stockings as he dragged it upward, high enough to discover the garters she wore. Sexy, impractical, lacy garters. The kind he loved to take off a woman, the kind so few women wore these days. Heat pooled at the top of his thighs, and he took her mouth with a deep groan.

Annie gasped beneath the pressure of Max's kiss. It astonished her...how could something be so exhilarating and frightening at the same time? Yet even as the thought formed, her head instinctively dropped backward, giving him better access to her mouth. She accepted the thrust of his tongue and the urgent pressure of his hands as they held her.

She could barely think, much less wonder why Max was kissing her after all this time, there were too many sensations cascading through her body.

He shifted, releasing his fierce hold for a moment, and Annie gulped. "M-Max?"

"Not yet," he mumbled. As a response it didn't make sense; it didn't even seem to be directed at her.

Annie frowned. *"Max?"*

"Shhh." His teeth caught her lower lip, nibbling gently, and it no longer seemed to matter. Max nudged her knees apart and she felt him against her inner thighs, the hard muscles of a man's legs in a place she'd never felt them before.

His mouth consumed her again, and she squirmed as desire bit deep into her abdomen. This certainly wasn't floating or shimmery, the pleasure was so wild it defied understanding.

Do something, urged her feminine instincts.

Annie raised her arms and hooked them around Max's neck, arching into his chest. It felt so good she moaned, the sound lost in their deep kiss. There was still enough sense in her addled brain not to wrap her legs around his hips, though her instincts were all for such a bold move.

Across the yard Grace's porch light came on, then her door opened, an event that registered at the edge of Annie's awareness. But she wasn't ready to abandon Max's arms, or the kiss that seemed to join them so completely she didn't know where she stopped and he began.

"Is that you, Max?" called Grace. "I heard the car."

"Yes...I'm here." His voice was so harsh that Annie barely recognized it.

"Have you decided to spend the night?"

Have you decided to spend the night?

Max shuddered, resting his forehead against Annie's. His grandmother's innocent inquiry raised all kinds of images—few of which involved spending the night in his childhood bedroom. His body wanted to sleep with Annie, though he was certain they'd get damned little sleep. But his mind knew it would be a mistake, the kind he'd always regret.

"Are you staying?" prompted Grace. Through the thick tangle of wisteria vines that shielded their embrace from view, Max saw his grandmother step out on her porch.

"No," he called quickly. "I'm going back to the city. I was just...telling Annie goodbye. I'll see you tomorrow."

"Are you still coming out tomorrow?"

"Yeah. For church and the ice-cream social. Good night."

"That would be lovely. Good night, dear." Grace disappeared back into her house.

Max would have said something then to Annie, but he drew a deep breath, inhaling the fragrance clinging to her hair and skin, and he knew he wasn't ready. He gently rubbed his lips over hers and she opened them readily.

It was plain Annie didn't have much romantic experience, and she certainly didn't understand the confused workings of modern dating, yet it was equally certain she had a natural talent at exciting a man. The sweetly eager way she kissed was a revelation in more ways than one—one more gift of her generous spirit.

His fingers were actually tangled in the complicated straps of her dress, trying to figure out a way to touch the rich curves beneath, when he froze. There were some boundaries he couldn't cross and still be able to face himself or Annie. He wouldn't be able to look her in the eye if things went as far as his body wanted him to go. She hadn't asked him to initiate her into sex, just to teach her something about clothes and dating.

Max tipped her head back, searching her eyes in the shadows. Did she ever plan to stop him?

"Annie?"

"Yes, Max?"

Still struggling with the heat in his blood, Max freed his hands from her velvet bodice and stepped backward. "You wanted to know about kissing," he said roughly. "A lot of men wouldn't have stopped at that point. You can't be too careful, Annie. Remember that, when you go out with your sheriff and schoolteacher. Don't trust the wrong guy."

Annie blinked. Stop? Why would she want a kiss to stop when it felt like that?

"Do you understand?" he persisted. "That was an inexpensive lesson. If you'd tried that with another man, you might have been sorry."

Her eyes narrowed. Lesson? Is that what Max thought he'd been doing? Giving her a lesson?

Well, she had a lesson or two for him.

Chapter Six

"Why, thank you, Max. That was so kind of you." Annie's voice dripped sarcasm, but she was too mad to care. "That's certainly a lesson I needed."

Max gave her a cautious look. "I just thought you should know."

"You thought *I* should know? In the first place," she said, jumping from the porch railing and poking her finger at his chest for emphasis. "I don't consider that I started that kiss. You're responsible for it, not me."

"You did start it."

"No, I didn't! I gave you one kiss, that's all. Then I stepped back. You're the one who decided I needed some stupid lesson about kissing and men getting carried away with themselves."

"It wasn't stupid."

"Yeah, right." Annie bit on the inside of her mouth so hard she drew blood. She'd finally gotten to kiss Max, then it turned out he was just teaching her a lesson about men taking advantage. While she'd wanted help on how to start dating, she didn't think she'd needed *that* particular lesson.

"It wasn't stupid," Max insisted again. "You wear a dress like that and then kiss a guy out of the blue, what do you expect?"

"A gentleman," she shot back. "And there isn't one thing wrong with my dress. It hardly shows anything. Honestly, you're impossible. For a big-city guy you're sure a prude."

"Prude? That's rich—you're the one who's still a virgin."

That hurt, though it shouldn't have. After all, it was true. She *was* a virgin. "That doesn't mean I'm a prude." Hard as she tried, Annie couldn't keep the hurt from her tone, and she heard Max sigh.

"Sorry, Annie. I shouldn't have said that."

"No, you shouldn't have." She wasn't ready to forgive him, not after getting all heated up, only to hear such an insulting reason for kissing her that way. "I may not have much experience with sleeping around, but I'm not quite as foolish as you seem to think."

"I don't think you're foolish, just…innocent. You don't know how men are."

"Believe me, I'm learning fast," Annie hissed. Right now there was one particular man she wanted to string up by his thumbs—or by any other convenient appendage he might have.

"Okay, I'm sorry. I shouldn't have done it."

Annie didn't mind that he'd kissed her, she minded the reason. But she couldn't say it without making things worse, and she was still furious, so she latched on to something else Max had said.

"Besides, I told you, the sheriff and schoolteacher aren't 'mine.' You seem to be having some trouble remembering the point of these little 'lessons' you think you're teaching me. I want to fall in love, not catch some guy who can't run fast enough to get away."

"Ann—"

"And exactly what is wrong with my dress? You don't like anything that doesn't cover me like a gunnysack."

"The dress is okay."

"You said, and I quote, 'You wear a dress like that and then kiss a guy out of the blue, what do you expect?'"

Max winced. "It just that I'm not used to you wearing sexy stuff. It surprises me."

"What surprises you? The fact that I'm wearing something attractive, or that I might actually *look* attractive."

A long time ago one of Max's stepfathers had taken him ice fishing in an effort to bond with him. It had never seemed worth the trouble to bond with one of his stepparents since they were never around for long, but he still remembered that day with crystal clarity. He remembered the silence, broken only by the sound of ice cracking beneath his feet, knowing that with each step, frigid water was waiting to swallow him whole. It was the way he felt now with Annie.

He cleared his throat. "You've dressed a certain way the entire time I've known you. Now you're wearing things that aren't…like that."

"Ohhhh." The filtered moonlight wasn't enough to reveal Annie's expression, but Max could see her rigid posture and realized he'd blundered again...though he didn't have a clue what the blunder might be.

Well, hell. He'd never claimed to be good with relationships. He didn't know what to say to Annie. Things weren't comfortable with her any longer, and that's when he usually said goodbye to a woman.

But he didn't want to say goodbye to Annie. Not now. Not ever. Surely they could get back to the easy friendship they'd always had before she'd decided to change her life by finding herself a husband so she could have a baby.

"You look great in your dress," Max said, trying again. "But you also look different, and it makes me uncomfortable, that's all."

"Oh." This time Annie didn't sound quite so angry.

"I guess I feel like a protective big brother."

Liar, taunted his inner self. He didn't feel the least like Annie's brother. For a brief, searing moment he'd felt like a lover, and he was still shaking from the close call. Annie would obviously be a fabulous lover, but she was a *marrying* kind of lover. He could never take her to bed without a wedding ring on her finger, which was probably the main reason he'd never seen her as anything but a friend.

Annie was still silent, though it wasn't clear whether she was angry or thinking or ready to cry.

"I'm sorry, Max," she said suddenly, sounding so calm that he frowned. "I thought you were teaching me how to kiss as part of our practice date. And since

I thought I was doing pretty well, it was disappointing to hear you had a different reason. I apologize for overreacting.''

"Uh, that's okay," he muttered, once more sensing an icy void opening under his feet. Much as he didn't like knowing he'd gone out of control with Annie, it was worse thinking she'd gone along with the kiss for "practice." A woman's first kiss was supposed to be special. Anyway he looked at it, he'd screwed up royally.

A headache twinged in Max's temples, so he pulled his keys from his pocket and motioned toward the car. "It's getting late. I'd better start home."

"It isn't that late. I thought city dwellers were night owls."

"Sacramento isn't like other cities. Remember what they call it? The biggest small town in the world," he said, repeating an old adage about California's state capital. Sacramento was a good-size city, but in many ways it had a small-town flavor.

"I prefer my own small town," Annie said stubbornly.

She plainly wasn't giving an inch on anything, and Max gritted his teeth. Annie had touched more than one raw nerve since announcing her intention of finding a husband. It wasn't just her new clothing that made him see her in a whole new way; she was changed in other ways, as well.

It was as if she was more...Max searched for a description, but the only one that came was *honest*. Not that she'd ever lied to him, but he had an uneasy feeling she'd hidden part of herself—the part that spoke her mind and didn't avoid arguments.

"Well, see you tomorrow. I'll take you and Grandmother to church," he said, hastily backing down the porch stairs. "Good night."

"Good night, Max."

He was halfway to Sacramento before he remembered that he hadn't checked the house before leaving. Annie's *un*locked house. The house that needed new keys and locks for the windows. Hell, he hadn't even waited to see her safely inside the door. "Damn," he growled, making a swift U-turn.

Annie had been coming home to a house she didn't lock her entire adult life, but he wasn't that casual about her safety. At least...he wasn't when he was thinking straight.

The BMW purred to a stop in front of the house, and Max jumped out. He started to knock on the door, then heard a soft peal of laughter coming from the backyard.

Annie.

She had a laugh that was warm and rich and made you feel good just to hear it. Silently he walked around the porch and stood in the deep shadows, watching her play in the sprinkler. She'd taken off her velvet dress and was wearing a white nightgown. In the silver moonlight she looked like a water nymph, too beautiful and otherworldly to be real.

Something brushed against Max's leg and he glanced down. It was Annie's rabbit, chewing on his shoelaces. He pulled his tie from around his neck and settled into one of the Adirondack chairs Annie had gotten the previous summer. Reaching down, he hefted the animal onto his lap.

Play **LUCKY HEARTS** for this...

exciting FREE gift!
This surprise mystery gift could be yours free

when you play **LUCKY HEARTS!**

...then continue your lucky streak with a sweetheart of a deal!

1. Play Lucky Hearts as instructed on the opposite page.

2. Send back this card and you'll receive 2 brand-new Silhouette Romance® novels. These books have a cover price of $3.50 each in the U.S. and $3.99 each in Canada, but they are yours to keep absolutely free.

3. There's no catch! You're under no obligation to buy anything. We charge nothing—ZERO—for your first shipment. And you don't have to make any minimum number of purchases—not even one!

4. The fact is thousands of readers enjoy receiving their books by mail from the Silhouette Reader Service™. They enjoy the convenience of home delivery...they like getting the best new novels at discount prices, BEFORE they're available in stores...and they love their *Heart to Heart* subscriber newsletter featuring author news, horoscopes, recipes, book reviews and much more!

5. We hope that after receiving your free books you'll want to remain a subscriber. But the choice is yours—to continue or cancel, any time at all! So why not take us up on our invitation, with no risk of any kind. You'll be glad you did!

Visit us online at
www.eHarlequin.com

The Silhouette Reader Service™—Here's how it works:

Accepting your 2 free books and gift places you under no obligation to buy anything. You may keep the books and gift and return the shipping statement marked "cancel." If you do not cancel, about a month later we'll send you 6 additional novels and bill you just $2.90 each in the U.S., or $3.25 each in Canada, plus 25¢ shipping & handling per book and applicable taxes if any.* That's the complete price and — compared to cover prices of $3.50 each in the U.S. and $3.99 each in Canada — it's quite a bargain! You may cancel at any time, but if you choose to continue, every month we'll send you 6 more books, which you may either purchase at the discount price or return to us and cancel your subscription.

*Terms and prices subject to change without notice. Sales tax applicable in N.Y. Canadian residents will be charged applicable provincial taxes and GST.

BUSINESS REPLY MAIL

FIRST-CLASS MAIL   PERMIT NO. 717   BUFFALO, NY

POSTAGE WILL BE PAID BY ADDRESSEE

SILHOUETTE READER SERVICE
3010 WALDEN AVE
PO BOX 1867
BUFFALO NY 14240-9952

NO POSTAGE
NECESSARY
IF MAILED
IN THE
UNITED STATES

If offer card is missing write to: Silhouette Reader Service, 3010 Walden Ave., P.O. Box 1867, Buffalo, NY 14240-1867

A dark nose wiggled at him, then sniffed his fingers.

"Be still," Max whispered, not wanting to distract Annie as she danced in and out of the silver streams of water, playing the impetuous game he'd seen a hundred times when they were children. She'd never been able to set out the sprinklers without being tempted into play.

But the game had changed, because this was a grown woman, lifting her arms above her head, swaying sensually, dancing to a music only she could hear.

The spiraling sprinkler circled, periodically making an abrupt switch in direction, gradually soaking Annie to the skin. The thin fabric of her gown clung to her skin, and she laughed as she gathered a length of it in her hands and wrung out the excess water, only to be sprayed again with another twist of the sprinkler.

Though Max had known Annie's figure was better than average, the silvered outlines of her body, tightened with the water and cool evening breeze, knocked the breath from his lungs. He'd touched her, kissed her, damned near made love to her, and his body was still hungry for the soft warmth that beckoned him, without her even knowing he was there.

"What am I doing?" Max breathed, closing his eyes. It didn't help—the image of Annie was seared into his brain and he could see her just as plainly.

He felt like a Peeping Tom, watching her like that, and he certainly needed the equivalent of a cold shower. But if he joined Annie while she played, or even let her know he was there, he was afraid of what might happen.

Curses hammered through his head as he got up,

put the rabbit in the chair behind him, then slipped into her house. He swiftly went room to room, checking that nothing was amiss, then went out the front door.

For several minutes Max sat with his fingers curled around the steering wheel of the BMW, fighting the desire clawing at him. A long time ago he'd resolved never to let his body make decisions for him. Passion was fine, but he couldn't let it control him; the cost was too high. Yet he couldn't remember ever having so much trouble controlling the need in his blood or the hard pressure behind the zipper in his slacks.

For Annie.

How could he have kissed and touched her like that?

"Get a grip," Max growled as he started toward the city again. He could ruin everything between them if he wasn't careful.

If his parents' many marriages had taught him one thing, it was that romance didn't last. And he'd rather have Annie permanently in his life as a friend, than lose her by becoming a lover.

The mattress shifted beneath Annie and she opened one eye.

"What?" She looked at the large brown rabbit watching her from the second pillow on the bed. "Jeez, Barnard. You startled me."

Barnard wiggled his mobile nose and didn't answer.

Naturally.

"I don't care if you *are* housebroken—I'd rather

find an honest-to-goodness man lying on that pillow. No offense intended.''

Barnard's chocolate brown eyes blinked, but he didn't look too offended by her comment. Probably because he'd prefer sharing his pillow talk with a nice lady rabbit.

"We're a fine pair," Annie murmured, reaching out and stroking her fingers through Barnard's soft pelt. "Are you lonely, too? Feeling a little lost and empty?"

It was the first time she'd really admitted the way it felt to wake up alone. And she wasn't thinking about making love, but the warmth of knowing someone was there, waiting for you to look at them and smile.

Someone like Max.

With a sad smile of her own, Annie closed her eyes again and cuddled deeper into the quilt around her shoulders. She'd never understood Max, but after last night she was even more confused. He'd kissed her so passionately, then he'd stopped as if it meant nothing to him. Right in the middle of everything he'd stopped and given her a lecture about trusting the wrong man.

"He's half-right," Annie muttered grimly.

Max was the wrong man for her. He might be sex incarnate, but she couldn't handle someone so confusing. Besides, he didn't want to live in Mitchellton, and it was her home.

"I'm not leaving Mitchellton," she told the rabbit. "And I don't care, anyway. He's a nice guy, but that's all." The protests sounded hollow, but she couldn't let herself care about Max in that way.

She had to face reality, and reality was that men like Max didn't fall in love with small-town girls who knew more about growing vegetables than haute couture. And Max wasn't planning to fall in love, period, so it was even more ridiculous to hope for something so impossible.

Barnard turned and hopped to the end of the bed, then jumped to the floor. Annie sighed. As a conversationalist, he lacked something.

A car that sounded like Max's BMW pulled into Grace's driveway, and Annie glanced at the clock. "Ten o'clock?" she screeched. She hadn't slept that late *ever*. Of course, she hadn't gotten much sleep, but ten? She had less than an hour to get ready.

Annie flung the bedding aside and dashed for the bathroom. Today was the first time she'd have a chance to meet the sheriff and schoolteacher wearing her new clothing.

"Get serious about this," she ordered her alter ego in the mirror. "Do you want to get married or not?"

The answer was a definite yes.

Fortunately she'd taken a long shower and washed her hair after playing in the sprinkler. It was one less thing to worry about in getting ready. Yet she froze when she spotted her wet nightgown...and the man's tie hanging next to it.

Barnard had carried the tie into the kitchen when they'd gone inside. His bunny teeth had eaten a ragged hole in the fabric and she'd recognized it as being the one Max had worn on their so-called date.

Annie lifted the tie and ran the thin strip of silk between her fingers, a small frown creasing the space between her eyes. She was certain Max had been wearing his tie when he'd left, so how had Barnard gotten hold of it?

He must have come back.

And he must have seen her dashing about in the sprinkler. A warm flush crept up Annie's neck, though not because he'd seen her doing something so silly as playing in the water. She always played in water, Max knew that. But the thin voile of the wet nightgown must have been transparent, even in moonlight.

Was that why he hadn't said anything? Just left again, without a word?

Hmm.

Another smile crept across Annie's face, though she couldn't have explained why it pleased her so much. Hadn't she decided Max was the last man she should think about? Wasn't he threatening her great plan to get married? She ought to have better sense than to wonder how Max had felt, seeing her next to naked.

Obviously, she didn't have a lick of sense, not when it came to Max Hunter.

A half hour later Annie took a deep breath and examined her reflection. Not bad. In fact, it was nearly as good as the velvet dress. She pirouetted in the mirror, loving the swish of fabric around her legs. The outfit might be a little fancy for a casual summer church service, but as the old saying went—all was fair in love and war.

Leaning down, she buttoned a single extra button on the slit up the skirt, the one Max had said was too revealing. She didn't agree, but she'd compromise since they were going to church together.

Peeking out the upstairs window, she saw Max standing in Grace's yard. He rubbed the side of his face, looking grim.

Well, fine.

He didn't have to be charming or anything. Their practice date was over, now she had to take things on her own. She'd promised Max she could manage, that she just needed his advice on getting started.

It was a promise she intended to keep.

Annie snatched her purse and rushed down the stairs—*not* because she didn't remember Max's advice on making her date come to the door—but because of it. The best way to get their friendship straightened out was to return to the way things were as quickly as possible.

"Hi, Max," she called in a deliberately cheerful voice as she walked outside. "Sleep well?" Yet even as the words left her mouth, Annie bit her tongue.

She shouldn't have brought up sleeping, though it was an innocent question—a question she'd asked him hundreds of times. But how did you act around a man you'd kissed so passionately? How did you relax and pretend everything was normal, when you knew perfectly well that nothing would ever be normal again?

"Fine."

"Well...that's good."

Max thrust his hands in his pockets and tried not to stare at Annie. She was wearing the dress he'd protested about, and he knew there was a touch of defiance in her choice. He wasn't really forgiven for the fiasco that had ended their date, and he couldn't actually blame her.

Hell, *he* was the one with experience. He should have kept things from going that far.

No woman wanted to hear she'd been kissed as a "lesson." And that was his excuse, not the true reason. The worst part was knowing he could have fixed things by admitting what a fabulous kisser she was. Of course, that would have carried its own pack of trouble, but he could still say it.

"Annie, I—" The words stuck in Max's throat.

"Yes?"

"I've been thinking about something." He stopped again, remembering his thoughts about her keeping part of herself hidden from him. It was a toss-up as to which subject was hardest to discuss. "The other day...you said I didn't like women who argued."

"You don't," she said reasonably.

"Is that why you don't argue with me?"

Surprise darkened Annie's eyes, but she just shrugged. "Seems we've been arguing a lot lately."

"Yeah, *lately*." Max put more emphasis on the last word than he'd intended, but he needed to understand. With most people it wouldn't make a difference one way or the other, but Annie wasn't most people.

Annie sighed. "What did we have to fight about before? It's not like we talked about anything that important."

"Of course we did. We're friends."

She glanced into the garden, mostly he suspected to keep him from reading her expression. "We play Trivial Pursuit and debate current politics. We talk about baseball and architecture and my plans for the garden—some about Grace, too, but mostly about little stuff.''

Without being told, Max suddenly understood what she was trying to say to him. In the past women had accused him of having trouble with intimacy, but this was the first time it mattered. And he understood something else: he didn't want Annie to change because there was less risk of losing her that way. If they never fought or screamed or got emotional with each other, there wouldn't be any reason to end their friendship.

Except…maybe he wasn't the kind of friend a woman like Annie needed.

"God," he muttered, sick to his stomach. "We never even talked about your dad…about the way you felt when he got sick. And then later.''

When you lost him.

Even now he was having trouble saying the things that should have been said when she was a grieving woman-child, left alone except for friends and a small town that lovingly took care of its own.

Annie looked back at him, and there was compassion in her eyes. "It's all right, Max. I understand.''

All right?

It wasn't all right with him, so how could it be all right with her?

"I'm sorry I wasn't there for you," he said. "I'll try to do better.''

Even as the words left his mouth, Max knew he'd have trouble keeping that promise. If she married someone else, her husband might object to her being friends with another man. Would their friendship survive? Could he stop being selfish and help her find a husband as quickly as possible?

Maybe. At least he could try. But he couldn't let her experiment alone; she was too naive. He'd have to stay around to protect her. Not too close, just close enough to make sure she didn't get carried away with her manhunting project.

And considering the way she'd blossomed, it wouldn't take long for some guy to tumble head over heels in love with her. The men in Mitchellton weren't blind, and they certainly weren't slow when it came to a pretty woman. He couldn't imagine the new sheriff or teacher would be any different.

"I'm really sorry," he muttered again, wanting to apologize for all the times he'd thought he was being a friend, when all he was doing was protecting himself. Yet she'd given him one chance after another—chances he didn't deserve.

"You were there, Max," Annie said softly. "You helped down at the store when Daddy was sick, though it would have been more fun to hang out with your buddies. You took care of the yard and made me laugh. You were there in your own way."

It was a generous thing to say, but Max knew he hadn't done enough. Annie was his best friend; she should have been able to talk to him. He was only just realizing how deeply she felt about things, and how much a woman like that must need someone special to share her life.

"I'm not doing any better now," he muttered. "Look how badly I handled things when you said you wanted to get married. About your problem...with having children."

"Don't worry about it, Max."

Annie put her hand on his arm, smiling sweetly, and his breath caught. Her hair was piled loosely on top of her head, and the dress was utterly feminine. She reminded him of the timeless beauty of a Gibson-girl photograph…a look he'd always admired. Of course he'd always thought she was pretty, she hadn't needed to dress up fancy for him to see it.

"All ready to go?" asked Grace Hunter as she walked around the corner of the house. "Oh, my," she exclaimed when she looked at Annie. "You look just fine, child. You'll have Parker and Josh wrapped around your finger in two seconds. It's going to be a very interesting Sunday."

"*Who* are Parker and Josh?" Max demanded.

"Do you really think they'll notice?" Annie asked, ignoring him.

"I never say things I don't mean. Mind my words, you'll be married by Halloween."

"*Who* are Parker and Josh?" Max said loudly.

"Parker McConnell is the new coach at the high school," explained his grandmother. "And Josh Kendrick is our new sheriff. Neither of them is engaged or has a girlfriend," she added.

Max frowned. "How do you know that?"

"I asked, of course." Grace shook her head and shared a commiserating smile with Annie as though her grandson was mentally deficient and they had to be patient with him.

He snorted. "So they must suspect somebody is doing some matchmaking."

"Handsome men like Josh and Parker *always* have somebody matchmaking for them," Grace said comfortably. "But they're fine young men and one of them will make a fine husband for Annie. Oh, that reminds me, did you get your cake to the church for the social?" she asked the younger woman. "It may be old-fashioned, but I still say the best way to a man's heart is through his stomach."

Annie nodded. "I put it in the church refrigerator yesterday afternoon. I changed my mind about the tiramisu, and made chocolate decadence instead."

"Perfect. That's the recipe that got grand prize at the fair for the past six years," Grace said, obviously pleased. "Well worth the trouble."

Max cleared his throat. "Let's get going. You don't want to be late for church, do you? Or for Josh and Parker," he whispered into Annie's ear, already struggling with his decision to support her manhunt.

It was one thing to think about her falling in love with some theoretical guy, but now he knew their names—Josh and Parker—and that his grandmother thought one of them would make Annie a "fine husband."

Not to mention the fact that Annie had made her prizewinning dessert for two men that Max already wanted to flatten.

Annie folded her fingers together and tried to listen to the sermon instead of thinking about her own problems. But it was nearly impossible. She had Grace on one side and Max on the other with his arms crossed squarely over his chest. Across the aisle sat the sheriff, Josh Kendrick, and a little farther down was Parker McConnell.

Josh and Parker had definitely noticed her, but each

time they'd come near her before the service started, Max's face turned into a thundercloud. An outsider might easily think he was jealous, but Annie knew better. He was just being difficult.

Still, both men had caught her gaze several times and were sending smiles her direction...smiles that were unmistakably warm and friendly. She was sure they'd ask her out if Max would just go away.

When the service was finally over and Grace had left to talk with some friends, she leaned over and whispered into Max's ear. "Go away. I can take things from here."

He gave her a wounded glance. "I promised to help you out."

"This isn't helping."

"Nonsense—it's good for them to think they have competition. Trust me. It's a male thing."

A low, wordless growl came out of Annie's throat. She wanted to smack him, but she didn't because they were in church and it wouldn't look good. "Max, I don't think you know what you're talking about."

"That really hurts. I'm a man, aren't I?"

"Well...yes."

"And you wanted my advice, didn't you?"

"Yes." It wasn't a lie. Although she'd had plenty of reason to question her judgement since asking him, in the beginning she *had* wanted his advice.

He patted her hand with avuncular patience. "Then take my word for it—men get all fired up when they think someone else is in the picture."

Personally Annie thought it was foolish. And she wasn't certain Max was reading the situation right. Maybe there was a difference between the way men acted in the city and the way they acted in a small town. Then she saw Josh Kendrick give Max a narrow glance, look at her again and move determinedly in their direction.

"Josh Kendrick," he said, holding out his hand.

"Annie James," she returned. Their fingers clasped in a brief, firm shake. She didn't get any electric tingles from the contact, but she liked the way it felt. "And this is my neighbor's grandson, Max Hunter," she said, trying to make the introduction as nonchalant as possible. "Max and I grew up next door to each other."

"Hunter."

"Kendrick."

The two men didn't shake, but they weren't openly hostile, so Annie tried to relax. "I heard about you rescuing that dog from the river," she said. "I'm impressed. A lot of people wouldn't have done anything, much less risk their life for a dog."

"It wasn't that dramatic. Besides, I love animals, Miss James."

"Hey, that's great," Max interjected. "Annie has the feed and seed store in town. She's an animal lover, too. You should see her rabbit and cat, they're really something."

Max winced when Annie dug her elbow into his side. Okay, so he was laying it on pretty thick, but this was hard for him. There didn't seem to be a single thing wrong with Kendrick, and he was definitely interested in Annie.

A sick sensation went through Max's stomach. Annie might well be married by Halloween, just as Grace had predicted.

* * *

"Ice cream, Sheriff?" asked one of the ladies in the serving line. She was sixty if she was a day, but she fluttered her eyes at Josh Kendrick like a girl of sixteen.

"Thanks, but I'll just have some of Miss James's chocolate cake," Josh said, smiling down at the woman by his side. "I hear it's legendary around here."

"It certainly is," the lady agreed. "Our Annie is a wonderful cook."

"I'm not old enough to be a legend," Annie protested.

"You certainly aren't." Josh took a bite of chocolate decadence and made an approving sound. "But this is worthy of a legend. It's delicious."

"Thank you." Annie grinned.

"I'll take some of that, too," said Parker McConnell. "If the sheriff hasn't hogged it all—the way he's been hogging your attention."

The two men smiled pleasantly, but Max could tell they were measuring each other, gauging their competition. They'd looked at him the same way before learning he was just a friend. Apparently, old friends didn't rate as competition, and it galled him. He was a man and they should worry about him the same as any other man. And he had known Annie for a long time, which meant he was closer to her.

"There's plenty for everyone," Annie said, taking the plate one of the servers handed to her and giving it to Parker.

"Thank you, Miss James."

"Please, call me Annie."

"Does that go for me, too?" asked the sheriff.

"Of course." Annie was thoroughly enjoying herself. Both Parker and Josh had been pleasingly attentive and openly admiring of her appearance. It was exactly the boost she needed.

"Annie is the best cook in the state," Max said.

Annie tensed. Every time she started to relax, he messed up her concentration by saying something or throwing her one of those enigmatic looks.

"Max, why don't you go sit with Grace?" she suggested.

"Naw, she's in the middle of a hen party and told me to go away the last time you sent me over there."

With an effort Annie kept from rolling her eyes. She ought to be annoyed over Max's description *hen party,* except that was exactly what Grace always called it.

"Then why don't you go get some more ice cream," she said.

"I've had two bowls already," he murmured.

If she had her druthers, she'd dump a bowl of ice cream over his head, but that wasn't possible, so she tried to keep smiling. Asking Max for help really *was* a mistake, though not for the obvious reasons. She'd always been aware of him, something she'd kept buried deep. But with Max acting so protective and downright impossible, it was hard to keep those feelings under control.

How was she supposed to fall in love with someone else if he kept hanging around?

She couldn't, that's what.

Max had to go away so she could get her head sorted out. Falling for a man who didn't want kids or believe in marriage wouldn't help her become a wife and mommy. It was a guarantee of a broken heart, nothing else.

"Hey, coach," shouted a couple of boys from across the room. "You'd said we'd have a practice this afternoon. Is that still on?"

"Er, yes, be right there," Parker called back. "It was lovely, Annie. I'll see you soon."

The sheriff seemed gratified at the other man's departure, but it didn't last. His cell phone rang, and he listened for a minute before throwing Annie an apologetic look. "Sorry," he said. "There's been some trouble out on the levee. I'll need to check it out."

"Gee, that's too bad," Max commiserated, unable to prevent an indecently pleased expression from crossing his face. "Hope it isn't serious."

"I doubt it." Josh gave him a hard look, plainly reassessing his role as a competitor. "Annie, may I call you? Perhaps later this week?"

"Yes...of course."

"Fine. I'll speak to you then."

As soon as he'd gotten out of earshot, Annie dragged Max to a quiet corner of the room and glared. "What do you think you're doing?"

"Helping."

"Next time help me from twenty feet away," she snapped, an annoyed pink flushing her cheeks. "Heaven knows what they thought with you hanging around that way."

"They thought you were a beautiful woman they wanted to date, that's what they thought," Max returned, equally annoyed. But he wasn't angry with Annie, he was angry with himself.

He'd decided to keep an eye on her from a distance, to help her marriage plan like a true friend, but he hadn't been able to stay away. As soon as the sheriff and the coach started circling, he'd gone nuts.

Which meant he had a real problem, because it was obvious that Josh Kendrick and Parker McConnell weren't going away. They'd be calling Annie, making dates with her, and there was nothing he could do to stop it.

Chapter Seven

"Do you really think so?" Annie asked, distracted by Max's certainty that both the sheriff and coach wanted to date her. It was one thing to think so herself, another to have someone else think so, too.

"*Yes.*" Max still looked like a thundercloud, but Annie decided to ignore it. He'd always been hard to understand, and lately he was downright confounding.

"I thought they were...it's just hard to be sure."

"You're a beautiful woman, why wouldn't you be sure?" Max asked, his tone softer now, more curious.

"You know." She shrugged and smoothed a lock of hair at her temple. No matter how many times she'd admitted her lack of experience to Max, she found it hard to say. "I know the clothes make me look okay, but—"

"Not the clothes, Annie." He gave her a steady look. "You've always been beautiful. The clothes just make a nicer frame, that's all. You were hiding before. Now you aren't."

Wistfully Annie wondered if that was true.

She supposed she ought to be insulted that Josh Kendrick and Parker McConnell had only taken a fancy to her now that she'd changed her appearance, but she wasn't.

At least...not much.

She *had* been hiding, not knowing how to dress right and afraid of looking silly. There must be a thousand tiny signals men and women sent to each other, saying they were interested or available, but she'd never been tuned in enough to send or receive them. She couldn't blame the two men for not seeing something she couldn't see herself.

But thanks to Max's help, she was learning. Which meant she shouldn't get so annoyed with him, even if she didn't always agree with what he thought was best.

She smiled brightly, trying to focus on her plan instead of Max. "You're right. I guess today went pretty well. Josh did ask if he could call me."

"It was okay." Max looked at her cautiously.

"I asked Grace over for lunch. Do you want to stay, too?" she asked.

"Yeah," he muttered. He didn't look happy, but Max looking unhappy was a common occurrence these days.

"All right." Annie hesitated, then edged away. There wasn't anything she could do to put things back to where they'd been...the place where they didn't talk about anything important except his grandmother.

Annie joined the other women as they cleaned up from the ice-cream social, responding to the familiar chatter with only half her attention. The self-recrimination in Max's eyes when he'd talked about her father's death still haunted her.

Somehow she'd never expected him to recognize the limits of their friendship, and now she wondered if it had been a mistake to guard her tongue whenever they were together...a mistake not to expect more from him. She'd just always respected the limits Max set down, knowing you couldn't change someone who didn't want to change.

"You sure drew some attention this morning," teased Eva Sanderson as they gathered the soiled dish towels for washing. "Nothing like a pretty girl to get a man active in the church. I think we'll be seeing a lot of those two gentlemen in the future."

"Two men? Don't you mean three?" asked Rachael Adams, the preacher's wife. "Max Hunter was so jealous I thought he'd start a brawl in the middle of the service."

The assorted women giggled, and Annie smiled obligingly. But it wasn't really funny; the idea of Max being jealous was crazy. He might have *pretended* to be jealous to help her catch Josh and Parker's attention, but it was all an act.

She tied the damp towels together and lifted the bundle, along with her empty cake platter. "I'll take care of the linens."

"But it's my turn," Rachael protested.

"That's all right. I need to do laundry this afternoon, anyway," Annie said, knowing she'd offered as an excuse to get out of the kitchen as quickly as possible.

She should have realized everyone would want to talk about the way she'd changed and the possibility

·

of a blossoming romance. There hadn't been a romance in the church since sixty-two-year-old, never-been-married Morris Jeppers had courted longtime widow Jane Hastings. Morris now had six stepchildren and fourteen stepgrandchildren that he doted on, but that was two years ago. Annie hoped there would soon be another happy story to talk about—one that included her name as part of a happily married twosome.

She stepped into the social hall, and Max came over and took the bundle of dish towels from her. It was a nice, almost husbandly thing to do, which only went to show how false outward appearances could be.

"Ready?" he asked. "Grandmother is waiting in the car."

"Sure."

Max put a hand at her waist as they walked out, the sort of protective, gentlemanly gesture that was old-fashioned and still kind of sweet. Annie sensed they were the center of attention of everyone left at the church and struggled to keep warmth from her cheeks.

Nobody would have thought anything of it before she'd gotten a whole new wardrobe. Now they watched her every move with a single man, even a single man like Max. The whole thing was ridiculous. Heck, he'd grown up in Mitchellton, and it wasn't any secret how he felt about marriage.

"Can you wait on lunch for a couple of hours?" he asked, apparently oblivious to the fascinated eyes fixed on him.

"Sure, but why?"

"The stores weren't open this morning, so I want to head back to Sacramento and hit a hardware place."

She blinked. "Hardware?"

"I'm going to install new locks at your house. Remember? Something better than those ancient skeleton key-locks you have right now."

"They aren't *that* old!" Annie said instantly. "And you won't do any such thing. I told you I'd take care of it, and I will."

"They're old enough," Max said, opening the car door. "And you can't get anyone to come out to the house today, so I'm taking care of it. You aren't going another day without proper locks."

"That's my concern, not yours," she retorted.

"Take my word for it, this is a fight you won't win," Grace said from the back seat. She gave Annie a sympathetic smile and shrugged. "Max is just as stubborn as you are."

"It's my house, not his."

Grace chuckled. "I gave him the same argument. He has this habit of not listening when he's made up his mind about what's good for you."

Max grunted and didn't say anything, which probably proved his grandmother's point. Not that he cared. He wanted Annie to be safe, and part of being safe was having a house she could lock against intruders. Even her precious sheriff would agree with him on this issue.

Her sheriff?

He scowled at the description, though he was the one who'd kept saying *her* sheriff, and *her* schoolteacher. They weren't Annie's yet, they were just men, one of whom she hoped to fall in love with. It was something she was insistent about—she didn't want any husband, she wanted a marriage based on love.

Annie wiggled in the seat next to him, the skirt falling away from her slender thigh, and Max swiftly refocused his gaze out the windshield. Whether she liked it or not, that dress was too revealing for Mitchellton. Either that…or he was the prude she'd accused him of being.

"You're being difficult," she said, fastening her seat belt. "I don't need you taking care of me."

"Did I say I was taking care of you?" Max asked.

"Don't be cute." They pulled out of the parking lot, and Annie waved at a group of churchgoers who were still standing around and visiting. "Everyone is probably in shock, seeing you two Sundays in a row," she commented.

"I'm sure they'll survive." Max lifted his own hand, acknowledging the reciprocal greetings. Most of the faces were familiar—older than he remembered from childhood—but otherwise not much changed.

"You're right—they survived your teenage years," Annie said flippantly. "They can survive anything."

Max glanced in the rearview mirror and saw his grandmother wearing a broad grin on her face. "Anything to add to that, Grandmother? You must have a thousand stories about my misspent youth, a few of which Annie may not have heard yet."

The older woman folded her hands in her lap, looking quite prim. "Not a thing. I just never heard you and Annie squabble before. It's educational."

"We're not…squabbling."

"Of course, dear."

Annie scrunched deeper in her seat and folded her arms over her tummy, refusing to meet Max's sideways glance. She knew Grace was trying to help, but it wasn't helping. The last thing Max needed was to be reminded of the way she'd argued with him for the past week.

Yet in a way it annoyed her even more. Deep inside she was itching to have a rip-roaring fight with Max. People disagreed; there was nothing wrong with it. She'd always held so much back with him...how could she be frank with someone *else* if she couldn't be honest with the one man she cared the most about?

The blood drained from Annie's face as she realized how perilously close she was to loving Max. Loving him the way a woman loved a man, not just as a friend.

No. She couldn't let it happen, couldn't open herself to that kind of hurt. When they reached the driveway to Grace's house, Annie had the door open before they'd even stopped moving.

"I'll see you later," she said over her shoulder, practically fleeing across the grass to the safety of her house. If she could have retracted the lunch invitation, she would have. But she'd already asked Grace, and Max had made up his mind to "protect her," which meant he would come to fix the locks no matter what she said.

Protection?

What a laugh.

She needed protection from Max, not from anyone else. He was the real menace in her life.

* * *

Annie swallowed as she watched Max.

It was a particularly hot day, the air holding a heavy stillness, which had led to him taking off his shirt while he worked. She might have appreciated the heat better if it had been any other attractive man in her house stripped down to his bare shoulders. But this was Max, and she was having enough trouble keeping some perspective without visual aids to distract her.

They'd eaten lunch, and Grace had gone to "take a nap," leaving Annie alone with Max while he fussed at her doors. He'd stopped at his condo and changed into jeans while getting the locks. He'd taken his shirt off after realizing the back door was warped and didn't completely close anymore.

The muscles had bunched and flexed across his shoulders as he pulled the pins from the hinges and lifted the heavy door out of the frame.

"Need to plane this down some," he'd muttered, a frown of concentration on his face. After setting the door on a couple of sawhorses, he shrugged from the shirt, wadded it into a ball and tossed it aside.

Max wasn't an exhibitionist, Annie was certain of that...but he ought to be. Her knees wobbled at the sight of his smooth chest and deep-bronze skin drawn over hard muscles. No tan lines on Max: he was just the way nature had made him, which was as nearly perfect as she could imagine any man looking.

"Get a grip," she scolded, sitting in the shade while he worked with her father's old tools. It wasn't as if she'd never seen Max without his shirt—there were plenty of times she'd seen him that way, including the time he'd installed the pond and fountains in the garden. But...it was the first time since he'd kissed her and she'd felt the power and strength of his body pressed against her.

As a lesson, Annie reminded herself. Maybe she'd look back on that evening someday and laugh—maybe when she was a hundred years old and totally senile.

When Max was satisfied with the door, he sealed the fresh-cut wood with primer left over from painting the kitchen and put it back on the hinges again. Every move was economical and assured, and it made her wonder.

"Max?" Annie said, resting her chin on her hand.

"Yeah?"

"How did you learn so much about repairing stuff? You're an architect."

He flashed her a smile. "I wasn't always an architect. I worked my way through Harvard as a construction worker."

"I thought your father paid for college."

Max kept his gaze on the new Primus lock he was installing and tried to ignore the way his gut tightened. His parents were never a comfortable subject. He usually did everything possible to keep from discussing them, but Annie didn't deserve to be brushed off just because she'd wandered into sensitive territory.

"Well, my dad was going to pay, but it turned out that he needed the money for another alimony payment."

"I'm sorry." Annie's eyes were dark and unhappy as she watched him. "You never said anything."

He shook his head. "Don't be sorry. Working construction gave me a much better appreciation for what goes into creating one of my designs."

"That's…nice."

"So it worked out for the best." Max put the pins in place and popped the doorknobs back onto the shaft before testing the lock. It turned easily and he nodded with satisfaction. He enjoyed designing new buildings, but there were times he needed to do something physical. He was one of those hands-on architects who probably drove contractors batty.

Annie watched for a while longer, then got up and stretched. As a concession to the heat, she'd put on a snug pair of shorts and camisole T-shirt top. Closely spaced tiny buttons stretched a path over her unfettered breasts and he wanted to pop each one open to see the firm curves beneath.

"Very adult," Max muttered as he marched into the living room to work on the door there.

Like his grandmother, Annie had never installed air-conditioning in the old farmhouse, and he wiped a trickle of perspiration from his forehead as he inspected the ancient door with attractive glass knobs on both sides. They were practically antique, and he doubted she'd appreciate him installing a modern set. That left drilling a new hole for a dead bolt, so she could lock the door that way.

"Does this help?" Annie asked softly, plugging in a large box fan and pointing the breeze in his direction.

A warm sensation crept around Max's heart, the sort of tender feeling that should have sent him running for the hills. He'd been thinking steamy thoughts about her all afternoon, fighting images of them rolling around, being sweaty together, but it was Annie's soft question that melted him the most.

"Perfect…thanks. You ought to go do something else. It's going to be loud when I start drilling holes."

He put his head down, determined to get his task done and escape as fast as possible. Annie was too sweet for her own good, and he tried to think of reasons her prospective grooms were wrong for her.

Problem was, both Josh and Parker seemed decent enough. His grandmother obviously approved, and Grace Hunter was an excellent judge of character. Both men were clean-cut and didn't act like kooks. Parker was fit and reasonably attractive if you liked the rugged all-American type. And the sheriff had the kind of rough good looks that women seemed to love.

The old drill whined loudly as Max positioned the bit. It occurred to him that in a few months Annie might be living here with her husband, a husband who would be using the same tools from the workshop he'd helped Annie's father build when he was thirteen.

If she got married, he wouldn't be using those tools again. He probably wouldn't be coming over for any casual suppers, and he certainly wouldn't be kissing Annie on the porch.

Kissing on the porch?

Where did that come from? He wouldn't be kissing Annie again, period.

Max was so distracted the drill slipped, nearly taking a chunk of his thumb with it. *"Damnation."*

Annie flew back into the living room. "Are you okay?"

"What do you think?" he snarled, waving his bruised digit in the air, then was instantly remorseful when she recoiled. He'd shouted from frustration—angry at his inability to let go of Annie, even in his mind.

"S-sorry. I'll get the first aid kit," she whispered, disappearing again.

"Ah, hell." He rested his forehead on the door frame. None of this was Annie's fault. He'd forced his so-called help on her, insisting he put new locks on the house. The only thing she'd *ever* asked him to do was advise her about clothing and dating, and he'd done that with ill grace.

"How bad is it bleeding?" Annie asked, returning with a bright-orange bag and opening it. It was a modern, fully equipped first aid kit, more complete even that the one he carried in his BMW in case of emergency.

"I'm all right. It's not bleeding at all," Max murmured.

"Let me see."

She knelt and took his hand between her much smaller fingers, inspecting the minuscule damage. He wanted to explain that it would take more than a brief encounter with a dull drill bit to get through his calluses, but her touch felt too good.

There were over forty thousand nerve endings in his hand and every one of them was responding to the way Annie gently traced each inch. The contrast of her peach-tinted skin and his much darker flesh did curious things to the pit of his stomach. He didn't even know how she felt about his Native American ancestry. It wasn't something they'd discussed, just another of those sensitive subjects he'd always avoided.

"I'm so dark," he breathed, spreading his fingers across her thigh. "Especially compared to you."

Annie's breathing stilled, then grew fast and shallow. A hard smile crossed Max's face. She might have returned his kiss because she was practicing her feminine skills, but at some level she responded to him.

"You know I can't get a tan," she murmured. "No matter what, I just stay the same."

"Same here."

Blood gathered low in his body, thick like the oppressive afternoon air. His hand was close to the most feminine part of her, the sweet warmth he was beginning to crave more than breathing.

It confused him, wanting her so much and knowing there wasn't a future in it, for either of them.

"Your skin is beautiful," she whispered.

"Is it?"

Annie nodded, keeping her gaze focused on Max's strong fingers; it seemed so intimate having him holding her thigh like that. He was in such a strange mood, it didn't make sense the way he was acting.

"One of my grandfathers was Apache," Max said. "That's where my dark coloring comes from."

"I know. Grace told me."

"It bothers some women, fascinates others," he said in a voice devoid of emotion.

She looked up, seeing the closed expression that she knew so well, the expression he got when Max was putting up barriers, telling the world to stay away. It turned his eyes to an inky, angry black. The first time she'd seen him that way it had frightened her, but she'd learned since then that it meant he was hurting in a deep place no one seemed able to reach.

"I understand why a woman would be fascinated with you," Annie said, picking her words carefully. "After all, you aren't the ugliest man in the world."

You aren't the ugliest man in the world.

A surprised laugh burst out of Max's throat. "Thanks."

Annie smiled back, feeling more comfortable, despite the masculine fingers still resting on her leg. She wasn't sure why they were on her leg, but she liked it. "I've always thought your Native American blood was part of the reason you're so attractive."

"Then it doesn't bother you?"

"Why would it bother me?" she asked, confusion crinkling her forehead.

"Why indeed?" Max touched the tip of her nose and smiled. "Have I mentioned how much I like you, Annie James?"

Annie tried to be glad that he'd moved his hand, but she wasn't. Men were hard to figure out, and Max had to be the worst of the bunch.

"Uh, would you like some lemonade?" she asked.

"Because I'm not bleeding to death?" He flexed his hand, and she blushed, having forgotten what had brought her to the living room in the first place. "Lemonade sounds great."

"I'll make some."

Annie grabbed the first aid kit and hurried to the back of the house, where she took a number of deep breaths and scolded herself for not using better sense. Things were happening so quickly, her senses awakening, her feminine needs more demanding than she'd ever thought they could be.

And Max kept hanging around, refusing to go away, confusing her.

One way or the other she would have to find a way to make him stay in Sacramento. Honestly, he'd spent more time in Mitchellton over the past week than in the past two months.

In the meantime she needed to make lemonade.

Still breathing raggedly, Annie pulled the old juicer from the cupboard. Most everything in the kitchen was old. Herbs grew in two cracked mustache cups dug up from the garden. She had the milk-green glassware her mother had collected before she was born, along with sixty-year-old cast-iron skillets and dutch ovens. She liked it that way. The store wasn't a big moneymaker, but her needs were simple, the house paid for, and she was able to save every month.

Soon the fresh, sharp scent of lemons filled the air, competing with the sultry heat. Max liked his lemonade on the strong, sweet side, so she added more sugar and juice than when she made it for herself.

"Brother," she mumbled, putting ice in the pitcher. "How can a woman know exactly how a man likes his lemonade and still know nothing at all about him?"

There wasn't an answer, and she sighed.

Max was testing the front lock when she returned. "Almost done?" she asked, handing him a tall glass.

"Almost." He smiled his appreciation and took a long swallow. "God, that's good. No one makes lemonade like you."

"I'm telling Grace you said that."

"Brat."

Max grinned over the lip of his glass. As a kid he'd had plenty of wild moments that would have made good telling—ones his grandmother knew nothing about—but Annie had never told, though she'd threatened plenty. She was the most trustworthy person he knew.

"I'm finished with the door locks, but I still have to check the windows," he said. "I want to be sure they're okay."

"It really isn't necessary. You've got more important things to do than worry about my windows."

"Nope." Max honestly couldn't think of a single thing more important than making sure Annie was safe.

"But—"

"Forget it, Annie. But I'd love another glass of lemonade," he said, handing her the glass. It was the quickest way to stop her from objecting to something he'd do anyway.

She frowned, but took the glass. "You're impossible."

"I know."

Grinning, Max went back to work. It didn't take long, the windows being in better shape than the doors. They had old clamp locks, most that still closed the way they were supposed to. The one that didn't was easily repaired.

"Now, I want you to promise you'll lock up every night and whenever you leave for the store or anything," he said before leaving.

"Yes, Daddy."

"I mean it, Annie."

"Okay, okay." She wrinkled her nose at the keys he dropped into her hand. "But it seems silly. Nobody locks in Mitchellton."

"Too bad. I'll be back out on Saturday to take you to the carnival. Grandmother isn't going, so it'll just be the two of us. It won't hurt to have Kendrick and McConnell think we're dating," he added.

Annie sighed. Maybe Max was right. Maybe Josh and Parker *were* challenged by the presence of another man, but that didn't mean she could get anywhere with him hanging around constantly. And it put her heart in the worst kind of danger.

"That's all right. I can take things from here," she said confidently. "You don't need to waste any more time with me."

"I haven't been wasting my time," Max returned, sounding irritated. "Don't say that."

"Max—"

"Annie," he said, mimicking her tone. "I'll see you next Saturday. Wear something pretty. You want them to notice you, right?"

"Wear something...*urggh,*" she growled.

"But now that I think of it..." Max murmured, his voice dropping suggestively. "Since you're a knockout in anything you wear, it really doesn't matter."

Annie didn't have time to say anything before he put a hand behind her head and dropped a hot, anything-but-platonic kiss on her lips.

"Mmm, that was nice," he said, his tone low and gravelly. "See you Saturday."

He waved a casual hand behind him as he strode

out the door, the sun gleaming on his black hair and bronze shoulders. Annie sank against the doorjamb, her arm across her breasts, touching her mouth, and feeling more confused than ever.

Chapter Eight

You don't need to waste any more time with me.

Max punched his pillow and glared at the ceiling. He'd never considered spending time with Annie to be a waste, and it was extremely irritating to be brushed off so blithely.

Hell, she was just getting started with this crazy manhunt. He could still be plenty of help.

I can take things from here.

Huh. Annie was such an innocent baby when it came to men, she couldn't possibly understand everything a woman needed to know. She was too straightforward, too honest and kindhearted. A lot of guys would take advantage of that kind of sweetness.

Josh did ask if he could call me.

Max grabbed his pillows and threw them across the room. He didn't want Josh Kendrick to call Annie, any more than he wanted Parker McConnell to call, but it was inevitable. She was the same beautiful woman she'd always been, but now she glowed with confidence, the self-assurance of knowing she looked her best.

Right, he told himself.

But she still needed him.

"She needs me to lock her in her room," he muttered to the ceiling. It was a primitive response, the same instinct that had led him to kissing her again.

"No, no, *no!*" he growled.

It wasn't the same instinct at all. Instincts were supposed to keep you alive, or at least keep you out of tough situations, but kissing Annie a second time was an even bigger mistake than the first. Just then the alarm sounded, and Max hit the button so hard the clock went flying, made a funny sound when it hit the wall and died quietly.

"Good. I hated that clock."

He got up and went to work. Work was good, work helped you get your priorities straight.

Work didn't help at all.

By Thursday Max was ready to chew nails.

He'd snapped at his secretary so many times she was threatening to quit. His cleaning service *had* quit. And he was seriously considering finding another place to live. All of a sudden the condominium complex seemed so perfectly manicured and *boring* he couldn't stand looking at it.

"Here," said his secretary, throwing a real estate listing on the desk. "The last time you visited the property on page twenty-seven it put you in a good mood. Don't bother coming back if it doesn't work."

"Sometimes you forget who is working for who," Max grumbled.

"That's *whom*," Ellen corrected. Ellen Manzke was a shrewd lady with short, iron-gray hair who'd worked for him since he was a green-behind-the-ears associate. She'd moved to California when he'd opened his own architectural firm, and they both knew she wouldn't be quitting in the foreseeable future. She was also capable of kicking him out of the office until his mood had improved.

Well, hell.

He might as well take another look at the property. It was out on the delta, located on a bluff overlooking the river, just outside of Mitchellton. He could stop by Annie's store and see how things were going, maybe even take her with him.

See if the sheriff had called.

So he wasn't claiming to be a saint. Maybe the best way to control his feelings for Annie was to get her married as quickly as possible. He had an ironclad set of morals when it came to married women. She'd definitely be off-limits once she was wed to another man.

Max started having second thoughts about the wisdom of seeing Annie so soon when he pulled into the feed and seed store parking lot. But it was too late, and he really wanted to know if the sheriff had called.

"Annie?" he called, walking through the door. The first thing he saw was Tigger, lying on the counter in supine splendor. "Hey, Tigger. I owe you big for Buffy. She hasn't called once since you gave her that mouse."

Tigger yawned, and a purr rolled from his furry chest.

Annie came through a side door and froze when she saw Max talking to her cat.

She'd nearly succeeded in putting him out of her mind, so it wasn't the most reassuring thing in the world for him to show up unexpectedly. "Max."

"Hey, Annie."

He smiled, and heat washed through her body. Okay, so she hadn't entirely forgotten him, but there were limits to what a woman could stand. "What are you doing here in the middle of the week?"

"I came out to look at some property and wondered if you'd like to come along."

"Sure," Annie agreed without thinking. She couldn't remember Max ever coming down to Mitchellton on a weekday, but maybe he wanted a second opinion. "Bert," she called, and a man appeared at the warehouse door.

"Yup?"

"I'm going out for a while. Will you listen for the bell and help any customers who come in?"

"Sure thing, boss."

Bert disappeared, and Annie looked at Max again. His gaze played over her, and she couldn't keep from worrying about the way she looked and whether it was too…much. Or too little. She wore a sleeveless top, cut straight across the top of her breasts, with one-inch straps exposing her shoulders. It ended two inches above the top of her snug jeans and showed her navel. Tame by some standards but daring for her.

The funny thing was that business had picked up in the last couple of weeks. The farmers stopped more often, ordering things they normally got out of catalogs, and there'd been a run on pet supplies and garden products. She'd always assumed the old-timers didn't approve of a woman running a farm-supply business, but they didn't seem offended by her more feminine way of dressing. More intrigued. And they loved to tease, as well.

Of course, women had stopped, too, but she figured they were just curious to know how things were going with the sheriff and the coach, having seen their interest at church.

If things hadn't been so awkward with Max she might have asked him about it, but she couldn't bring up the subject without getting things mixed up again. They were already mixed up enough.

"Is this land for a client?" Annie asked after getting into Max's BMW. It wasn't until they were driving that she realized she hadn't thought twice about being "helped" into the car.

"Actually, I'm thinking about getting it myself. It's a great location—plenty of big old trees and a view of the river."

"A house...for yourself?" She kept the surprise from her voice with an effort.

"I haven't made up my mind. An investment, at any rate."

They turned off the main road onto a smaller road that Annie knew didn't go anywhere near the city, which made her more and more curious. Max was the last person she'd ever expect to be intrigued with a place in the country; he was more of a penthouse type of guy.

On a small rise of land was a house she'd seen a hundred times, but never from the inside. "You're buying the Mitchell house?" she gasped, delighted.

"I'm thinking about it. I've got an option on the property, but it runs out in a couple of weeks."

Max parked by the sagging steps of the porch, and Annie squirmed with excitement as he walked around to her side of car. "I've always wanted to see inside," she said, accepting the helpful hand he extended.

He winked. "Isn't that lucky...I just happen to have the key."

She laughed and followed him up the steps. She knew the history of the house, of course. Mitchellton had been named for the Mitchell family. It was one of the old delta homes built by the wealthy city elite as an escape from the summer heat, though it had suffered from neglect for several decades. What enchanted Annie was knowing that a devoted husband and wife, very much in love with each other, had lived there once upon a time.

The door swung inward, and Max gestured for her to precede him. Holding her breath, Annie stepped inside and felt enveloped by warmth and history.

"It's wonderful," she whispered, looking up at the grand staircase and the crystal chandelier still hanging above.

Max looked around, a faint frown creasing his forehead. It was a moldering old house, he couldn't see what was so great, not in its present condition. "I can't go wrong buying the land, that's for sure. But the existing structures will have to come down before I can develop."

Annie spun around, horror on her face. "You wouldn't."

"It's a wreck, honey. It's got to come down."

"Don't you *dare,*" she said fiercely. "This house is special. You can't tear it down."

He stared at her helplessly. As an architect he appreciated the old place, and it did have interesting features unlike other homes of the same era, but restoring a wreck in the backwaters of the Sacramento River delta was a foolish undertaking. He could never expect a profit that way.

"Annie, it's just a house."

"No. It's history and romance and passion. You just can't destroy it."

"It's history, all right," Max said, exasperated. "Prohibition history. The place was a notorious speakeasy."

"So it's a historic landmark."

"Not by a long shot. Do you have any idea of how much money it takes to restore something like this?"

"Is it worth restoring? I mean, is the foundation and stuff still good?" Annie demanded.

"Uh, yeah."

Max didn't like admitting it, but the structure was basically sound despite the years of neglect. And there was something else he wouldn't admit...deep down he itched to fix the sagging steps and begin replastering the walls. But it wasn't practical. His clients weren't interested in historic relics, they wanted the latest in modern amenities. The only sensible justification for buying the Mitchell property would be as an investment, which meant building a house he could sell to someone with money to burn.

"Max, please. Don't tear it down," Annie said, putting her hand on his arm. Her blue eyes were troubled, even anxious, and he sighed.

"Restoration—"

"You could do a lot of the work yourself," she interrupted eagerly. "You said you worked in construction during college. I'll bet you'd be great fixing it up. And I'd help."

"You won't have time to help," Max reminded. "You're getting married and starting a family."

Some of the light died in her face. "I'm not married yet, not even close. So I may never— You know." Annie shrugged diffidently, as if admitting she might never marry and have a child wasn't as painful as he knew it must be. But her eyes filled with tears, despite a visible effort to control them.

Damn, damn, *damn*.

Max pulled her into his arms and rubbed a soothing hand across her back. Life was full of emotional pitfalls, but he'd spent so much of his time avoiding those pitfalls he hadn't learned a single thing about dealing with them.

But Annie knew. She'd lost a loving father and had gone on with a grace and courage he was just beginning to recognize. And she'd go on if she couldn't have the baby she'd always dreamed of having. She'd hurt, but she'd get through it.

Annie's baby...

Something tight and painful squeezed Max's heart. Annie would be a wonderful mother. Her child would grow up loved and safe and confident, cherished no matter how many dirty fingerprints she found on the refrigerator. She'd go fishing and play in the sprinkler with her child and laugh when she was given a frog for Mother's Day.

A wonderful mother...and an incredible wife.

Max closed his eyes, smelling Annie's sweet fragrance, and wished he was different, wished he could go back to the beginning of childhood and believe in happy endings again. But even if Annie was the ideal wife, he was anything but an ideal husband. You had to believe in something to make it work, and he couldn't believe in marriage.

"You'll be a mother," he whispered, promising something he couldn't hope to make come true. "And a wife."

"Think so?"

"Yeah."

Annie let herself lean on Max, accepting the comfort he offered. She knew he didn't usually act this way; teary-eyed women *usually* made him run for cover. Then all at once she realized he might decide she was trying to manipulate him, and she squared her shoulders.

"Um...sorry," she apologized, sniffing a little. "This has nothing to do with the house."

"Of course not," Max said, looking at her curiously.

"But you aren't tearing it down."

"Hon, if I don't, someone else will."

"But..." Annie bit her lip and looked about the dimly lit room. The kindly ghosts in this house were silent for Max. He didn't have faith in love, not the kind that lasted, living forever, even after the body was gone.

But Annie believed.

She'd seen the grief in her father, his steadfast love for her mother. And she remembered his dying words, the light in his face despite the pain, because he was seeing her again. Annie didn't know if her mother had come, somehow, to be there in those final moments, but she liked to think it was true.

"As long as we're here," she said slowly, "let's take a look around."

"Okay." He fixed her with a stern gaze. "But you're not going to talk me out of tearing it down."

She gave him a sunny smile. "We'll see."

"Annie."

Annie recognized that tone. It was the voice Max used when he was exasperated…and willing to be talked into something he really wanted to do.

"Come on," she said, tugging on his hand. He probably hadn't looked that closely at the house, not if he was planning to tear it down. Surely he could see the potential of a place that had withstood time and the river for more than a century.

They wandered from room to room, surprised to find furniture in some of them, covered by dust sheets for protection. Much of the glass in the windows was still original, some of it beveled, some of it stained glass in beautiful patterns of wisteria and water lilies.

"That's Tiffany, isn't it?" she asked, using one of the sheets to polish decades of dust and grime from a particularly striking panel.

"More likely a good copy. The seller is offering the property lock, stock and barrel—contents included. I can't imagined they'd leave so much Tiffany glass behind. Not for the price they're asking."

"Mmmm. You never know."

Annie froze at the French doors of the conservatory, instantly falling in love. It was large, with crumbling wicker chaises for sitting by long-dry fountains and koi ponds. Her fingers itched to clean it out, to plant orchids and plants and vines to reach once more toward the high glass ceiling.

Max watched Annie's enthralled face and knew he was sunk. There was no way he could tear down this house, any more than he could let anyone *else* tear it down, either.

And he realized something else.

He'd brought Annie here because he'd known she would talk him out of it. He'd known she would reach that part of him that wanted to test himself, to repair something old and beautiful. The part that appreciated an earlier, unknown architect who'd built a house to last for generations.

Annie looked up from where she sat, stroking a brass frog sitting on a brass lily pad in the empty pond.

"Okay," he said. "The house stays. But you'll have to help. We'll consider it a trade...for helping with the dating thing."

She laughed and jumped up to throw her arms around him. "Thanks, Max. I knew you couldn't do it."

He still didn't know about the sheriff calling, but with Annie nestled close to him with that trusting expression in her eyes, it didn't seem so important.

Annie tugged at the neck of the sundress, uncomfortable with the idea of going without a bra *or* straps to hold the darn thing up. The dress seemed glued in place, held by the elastic stitching throughout the bodice, but she felt strange about it.

The doorbell rang, and Annie wrinkled her nose.

Max.

She was thrilled he'd decided against tearing down the Mitchell House, but she still wasn't sure about him taking her to the carnival.

With a last glance in the mirror, Annie grabbed a light sweater and ran downstairs. "You're early," she said, throwing open the front door.

Max frowned. "And you should ask who's there before answering the door."

"I knew it was you."

"Hmm." He pulled out a bunch of daisies from behind his back and presented it to her. "Here."

"Th-thank you." There Max went, doing something that made her all mushy inside again. And he looked perfectly scrumptious, sort of 1950s retro in his jeans, white T-shirt and leather jacket. Sinfully sexy. "I'll put these in water."

"Okay. Then we'll roll." Max grinned and hooked his thumbs in the belt loops of his jeans. He had a daring, brash expression on his face.

When Annie returned and followed him outside, she gasped at the sight of a perfectly restored 1965 Mustang in the place of Max's BMW. "Where did you get that?"

"A loan. Scratch it and I'm dead meat."

"Oh." Annie suppressed a giggle as she got into the low seat. With the Mustang, Max's assistance was a definite plus, and she imagined getting out would be even more of a challenge. "You're in a strange mood," she said as he folded himself into the driver's seat.

"I—ouch! I'm a little big for this car." Max rubbed his knee where he'd bumped it. "I can't take you to the prom, so you're getting a date to the carnival."

The gesture was so un-Max-like that Annie was astonished. "Oh...that's nice."

"But I'm the only one who gets to kiss you," he said firmly. "You can't volunteer at the kissing booth. A fellow's girl shouldn't do stuff like that."

He'd remembered.

Annie didn't take the part about kissing her seriously, but she was touched he'd remembered what she'd said about the kissing booth. And he was trying so hard to give her a night like the ones she'd missed as a teenager.

"All right. No kissing booth," Annie said meekly, though she'd never been meek in her life. Shy perhaps, but not meek.

"Right."

The Mustang roared to life, and Max peeled out of the driveway with precise skill, kicking up gravel and leaving a cloud of dust. It was reckless and exciting, and she dropped her head back laughing, but under the laughter was a thread of sadness. She had so much with Max...and so little.

She treasured each moment with him and knew there couldn't be many more. Not like this. It was too risky. Her heart was so confused now she didn't know how she could fall in love with *any*one. And she wanted to. Oh, how she wanted that.

The festivities were in full swing when they arrived at the high school. Over the years a lot of money had been raised at the carnival, money for the school system, with everyone throwing in to make the event as big as possible. There was even a small midway, with a Ferris wheel and roller coaster and other rides for daring people with strong stomachs.

Summer school students worked on the booths, each year feeling challenged to make them better than the last. This year the carnival was decorated with thousands of red, white and blue twinkle lights, and as the sun dropped, turning the day to twilight, everything sparkled gaily.

They'd ridden the roller coaster and tossed ping-pong balls at tiny bowls holding goldfish, now Max was trying to win her a teddy bear by throwing darts at balloons.

Annie clutched his leather jacket to her chest and ate pieces of cotton candy while she watched him pop one balloon after another. It took a lot of balloons to win a bear.

She'd forgotten her marriage plans for a blessed moment, then heard Parker McConnell's deep voice. "Annie...I hoped I'd see you here."

"It's good to see you, too."

Max looked over in time to see Annie give McConnell a friendly smile. He'd known they'd find her no matter how crowded the carnival might be. It was more than the lack of available women in a small town like Mitchellton; it was her sweet nature that fascinated men like Parker and Josh.

And him.

Suddenly angry, he threw down a ten-dollar bill, and in swift succession threw the fifteen darts it bought him. Each hit the target, burying the steel points a full inch into the board. He dropped a twenty in the pie-tin holder nailed to the rail in front of him.

"Whoa, man. Give us a chance to blow up more

balloons,'' said the kid tending the booth. He looked a little nervous, as if he should think twice before putting more sharp objects in Max's hand.

''Just give me the damn bear,'' Max growled, dropping four more twenties on the plate.

The kid's eyes brightened. ''I guess that's enough balloons,'' he said, scooping up the money and handing over the coveted stuffed animal.

Max stomped over to where Annie stood talking to the coach and pushed the bear in her face. ''Won it,'' he said.

''Thanks, Max.'' She cuddled the bear under her chin, and some of his ire faded...until he looked at Parker. The man had his gaze fixed on her with a predatory expression that Max, as another man, recognized all too well.

''Gosh, coach,'' Max drawled, ''hope the football practice went well last Sunday. You're sure starting early—the first day of school is a long time off. Checking out the best players?''

Parker looked surprised, then shook his head. ''The kids asked if we could have some early practices, but I'm really not one of those gung-ho coaches. It's more important for them learn discipline and good sportsmanship. And with such a small student body, everybody gets to play. To be frank, I prefer it that way— never liked turning a kid down for the team.''

Okay, Max had to give the guy points. Mitchellton wouldn't mind contending for the state championships, but with a student body of less than a hundred, it was unlikely. And Parker did seem to like children.

Max scowled harder.

He'd just made Parker McConnell look better to

Annie, which was something he hadn't intended to do. Dammit, there were limits to how much he could take. He ought to be glad a decent man was interested in her, but it was impossible.

"Well, we're headed over to ride the Ferris wheel," Max said, putting his arm around Annie's waist. "See you around."

Annie sent an incredulous look at him as he dragged her toward the line of kids waiting in line for ride tickets. "What do you think you're doing?" she asked.

"Going for a ride on the Ferris wheel."

"Parker—"

"I'm your date tonight, not Parker McConnell."

"Max," Annie said, obviously trying to sound patient. "This is very sweet of you, but we aren't really on a date, and Parker was being very friendly."

"Yeah, I caught that."

"I really can take things from here. You don't have to stick around so much."

"Like hell I don't."

Annie ground her teeth while Max plopped down money for the tickets. He was being completely unreasonable. It had to be a protective streak left over from their childhood. That abominable "big brother" attitude he'd talked about.

"Big brother," she muttered beneath her breath as they waited a second time in the Ferris wheel line. She didn't need a big brother, she needed a man to love her.

She needed…Max.

And that's what hurt so badly, because she wasn't going to get him.

"What did you say?" he asked, urging her forward with a hand on the small of her back.

"Nothing."

It was their turn, and they stepped into the narrow seat while the ride attendant clamped the bar down across their legs, then turned the wheel forward to load the next car. It was a modest Ferris wheel the town had bought decades ago, and the seats weren't generous. Swallowing, Annie realized how snugly they were pressed together in the narrow space. She tried to shift positions, but there wasn't room, and she shivered.

"Told you not to leave your sweater in the car," Max scolded. "Put my jacket on."

"Uh, that's okay. I'm fine."

"Now, Annie, don't be difficult." Over her objections he wrapped her in the jacket, then put his arm over her shoulders. "That's better. More room this way."

Annie squished her new teddy bear against her stomach. She'd never minded nursing her father during his illness, but she had to admit it would have been easier to figure out all this boy and girl stuff when she was a girl herself. As a grown woman it was embarrassing to be so ignorant.

The ride finally started, which meant it would be over soon, and Annie breathed a sigh of relief.

The relief didn't last.

Boisterous teenagers in the other cars were hollering and bouncing wildly in their respective cars, and she grasped the bar over her thighs. "What are they doing?"

Max shrugged. "Trying to stall the wheel. But they

aren't doing it right. They've got to coordinate that rocking motion to do any good.''

"How would you know?''

"I've stalled this particular Ferris wheel more than once. Nothing better than getting stuck up in the air with a pretty girl,'' he said with a wicked grin as the ride ground to a halt. "Yeah, that did it. And we got the best spot.''

They were at the very top of the Ferris wheel. If Annie hadn't been so nervous she would have appreciated how pretty the lights and color looked from so high, but she could barely think. Max was doing it again, acting possessive and loving and she couldn't handle it.

"Max, we have to—''

His strong fingers had caught her chin, and her protest was lost in a wordless kiss.

Chapter Nine

The ride began moving again, and Annie broke free, staring into Max's eyes.

"What are you doing?"

"Kissing you, what do you think?"

"I don't need any more lessons, thank you."

"It wasn't…" The protest died in Max's throat, because he hadn't kissed Annie for any other reason than he wanted to. No lessons, no lame excuses in his mind, nothing but the need to kiss her beautiful mouth. He wanted her so badly it was tearing him apart, but he wasn't the man she needed, could never be the kind of husband Annie should have.

The ride operator was ejecting the troublemakers, but when he got to Annie and Max, he grinned. "Guess you folks didn't have anything to do with that mess. You can stay on."

"Thanks, but we've had enough," Annie said, blindly trying to find the release on the protective bar.

She was conscious of the man's inquisitive gaze as he unfastened the mechanism and held the car steady for her to step out. Max caught up with her at the edge of the midway, catching her elbow and swinging her around.

"What's wrong?"

She tried to shake free. "Nothing."

Everything.

"Things are going fine now, Max. You don't have to worry about me," she said. "I'm going to dinner with Josh next week, and Parker asked me to go river rafting with him over the weekend."

"Just like that?" Max demands. "You hardly know them. How could you just accept?"

Annie glared. "How else do you get to know someone?" she demanded. "Of course I accepted. I wouldn't go out with a total stranger, but they aren't strangers. Why can't you be happy for me?"

"I am happy."

"Yeah, you sure act like it."

Annie spun and marched away from the carnival. Away from Max. Nothing was far from anything else in Mitchellton, she'd just walk home and forget the way her heart was tearing itself apart.

"Annie! Where do you think you're going?"

"Home."

He cursed behind her but she ignored it. Pretty soon the throaty purr of the Mustang crept up alongside her. Max stuck his head out the window.

"Get in, Annie."

"Go to hell, Max." She didn't usually use strong language, but he was bringing out the worst in her.

"You're being unreasonable."

"Well, that's the way women are. Good thing you don't have to worry about it, isn't it? I'm not your problem."

"You were never a problem."

"Fine."

She kept walking, though her new sandals were raising blisters on her feet. The discomfort was nothing to the way her soul felt, and it gave her something to think about—something other than the hurting that wouldn't go away.

"Dammit!" Max veered directly in front of her, and Annie turned onto the path that led down to Mitchellton's river park. He couldn't take the Mustang down there, and she doubted he'd leave the vintage car where somebody might have a chance to steal it. There wasn't much car theft in Mitchellton, but Max acted like the place was a hotbed of crime.

A few seconds later she was proved wrong when Max came storming down the path himself.

"Annie, you get back here."

A tight smile twisted her lips. She might be a small-town woman without much experience, but she wasn't someone he could order around. At the edge of the park she paused long enough to kick the sandals from her aching feet, then slid into the shadows of a spreading elm. She knew every inch of the park, something Max probably couldn't claim.

"Going somewhere?" he asked, abruptly grabbing her from around the rough trunk of a tree.

The scream that had instinctively risen, died in her throat. *"Max."*

"Thought you'd gotten away, didn't you?" he asked smoothly. "Thought I couldn't possibly know where you'd gone. You forgot this park is a teenage boy's favorite make-out spot. I know every dark corner like the back of my hand.''

"I wouldn't know about that," Annie snapped. "I never made out with a teenage boy."

"It's never too late," Max said, tugging her flush with his body. "Of course, we aren't teenagers, but we shouldn't let that stop us."

"Ohhhh," she shrieked. "Why can't you leave well enough alone? You don't really want me, you just want things to stay the same. You want me to be good old Annie. Comfortable. No complications. You want to show up when you don't have anything else to do and spend a few hours with someone who makes no demands on you."

"That isn't true."

"No?"

"No," he said, sounding annoyed.

"Then what do you want?"

Max didn't answer for a long time, then he put his forehead against hers and sighed. "I don't know, Annie. I honestly don't know. I used to want that…used to want what you said, but everything is changed now. I just don't know."

Her heart ached, recognizing the pain in Max's voice. There was more to being alive than a successful career and having a home in the city. He'd spent so much of his life avoiding the conflict he'd hated in his parents' marriages that he didn't know how to live.

"I can't stay in the past, Max."

"Just don't…go out with them. Please, Annie. Give me some time."

She sighed. "I don't think time is going to fix this."

He tugged her head backward, exposing her throat to his lips. Kisses trailed down to the throbbing hollow in her neck. The tip of his tongue touched the spot, and his breath washed over her skin, tightening her breasts.

One more time.

One more kiss. An embrace that was more than a lesson, more than a moment of confusion. A kiss meant for her alone. Annie moaned, knowing she shouldn't let Max have this much power over her. But it was too late and she'd wanted him for so long, deep in the recesses of her heart.

Max turned with her suspended in his arms, and beneath her bottom she felt the surface of the new fiberglass picnic tables that Mitchellton's volunteer fire department had donated to the park. *It sure took a lot of car washes,* she thought inconsequentially. Wooden tables would have been cheaper, but the guys had wanted the best, and that's what they'd gotten.

"Max…"

"No." His mouth fastened over hers with a fierce pressure, and his hands swept over her, demanding something she didn't understand. It was so sudden, so overwhelming, that she froze.

"I'm sorry, honey," Max whispered a moment later, loosening his grip. He'd frightened Annie and it was the last thing he'd wanted. He rubbed her back until she lost some of the tension his thoughtlessness had caused.

The distant backfire of a car brought Max's senses back to reality for an instant, and he lifted his head, listening. An owl hooted in the distance and the wind rustled through the trees, but there was nothing else.

"Everyone is at the carnival," Annie murmured. "Except Grace, and she's at home."

He looked down, wishing he could see her face in the deep shadows. She was lovely, so very different from the other women he'd known. And yet she'd always been there, wise beyond her years, generous and loving.

He kissed her again, shaking with need, though he would chop off his arm before frightening her again.

This time she kept her mouth closed, and Max smiled in the darkness. So innocent. So sensual. So many dizzying contradictions in Annie's slender body. Her complexity tempted him so much he was almost scared to touch her. He was beginning to suspect that while Annie had never left Mitchellton, he was the one who'd failed to see the world.

"It's too dark. I can't see you," he murmured.

"I look the same as always."

"Mmmm." Max put his fingers lightly on her face, touching the features he knew so well. He'd never done that before, why would he? They were friends, and friends didn't touch in the same way. But now he explored the curve of her eyebrows, the satiny warmth of her close eyelids, the delicate line of her jaw.

And her hair...Max breathed a prayer of thanks she hadn't wanted to change that part of her appearance.

He loved Annie's long hair.

The soft strands caught on his calluses, pouring like liquid silk across his hands, and he gathered bunches of it, relishing its softness, imagining how it would feel spilling across his body.

Then, leaning down, he traced the outline of her mouth with his tongue. Teasing. Tempting. Coaxing. Wanting her response as a gift, not something taken.

"Oh...Max," Annie sighed, opening her lips. His tongue stole between, tasting the lingering sweetness of cotton candy, exploring the warm recesses offered to him.

Max nearly lost it, his control threatened more than he would have thought possible. He'd kissed a number of women, but like everything else with Annie, this was different. *Better*. So much better it didn't bear comparison.

"You're so sweet," he breathed.

Annie trembled, shocked by the sensations spearing through her. She'd accepted that her ideas about making love were wrong, but she still wasn't prepared for the intensity, the way her body didn't seem to belong to her when he touched her. She didn't know how to handle the hungry feelings, the weakness in her legs, or the aching emptiness that was unlike anything else she'd ever felt.

The kiss went on and on until they finally broke apart, dragging air into their starved lungs.

"That—"

"I know," Max said.

He eased her knees apart, pulling her tight against him, and there wasn't any doubt of his response. Annie set her palms flat on the picnic table, resisting temptation. It would be so easy to unsnap his jeans, to pull the zipper down and explore those masculine contours.

Max rocked forward, pressing against her center, and she moaned.

"Do you like that?" he breathed.

Like it? How could she like something that was burning her alive?

With casual ease Max put his hands on her shoulders, let them slide downward, and with a quick tug on the elastic bodice of the sundress, pulled it down to her waist.

"No, don't," Annie gasped. She caught his wrists too late, he'd already found her breasts, caressing them, plucking at her nipples with expert care.

"Like velvet," Max breathed, playing with the hard points, rolling them between his fingers before dropping his face into her neck...and then lower.

A low cry escaped Annie's throat as Max drew her into his mouth, sucking hard. The exquisite pain at the top of her thighs grew unbearable, yet she couldn't stop reaching for it, arching into Max's body and cursing the clothes that separated them.

When he transferred attention to her other breast, Annie couldn't take it any longer. The heck with resisting temptation. She reached for the snap on his jeans and pulled it open.

Max groaned. He wanted Annie's hands on him more than he'd ever wanted anything, but it wasn't right. If she touched him there he wouldn't be able to pull back, he could barely stop now.

"Annie...no." He grabbed her fingers away.

"Max. Don't you want—"

"Hell, yes, I want. But that's where it stops."

Feeling battered, her body still thrumming with need and frustration, Annie scooted backward on the table. "Fine." She pulled her bodice into place, reflecting bitterly that she'd been right about the stupid sundress. She should have worn something with straps.

And she shouldn't have gone anywhere with Max Hunter.

"Don't you *dare* say you were teaching me a lesson," she hissed.

"I wasn't teaching anything. That was all me, wanting to kiss you."

"Well...fine." His admission took the wind out of her sails, but then she frowned. "If you wanted to kiss me, why did you stop?"

"Because I'm a gentleman!"

"Since when?"

"Since my best friend decided she wanted my help in finding a husband."

Annie's eyes narrowed. "We are not best friends, and I did *not* ask for your help in finding a husband, I...oh, forget it," she growled. It no longer mattered what she'd asked Max. She jerked the skirt of her dress down over her knees.

"Honey, please understand."

"Don't call me that," she said quickly. "I'm Annie. Just Annie."

"What's wrong with honey?"

"Nothing, if you'd ever called me that before."

"Sorry."

The sound of a zipper whispered through the darkness, followed by the pop of a snap being closed, and warmth crept into Annie's cheeks. She must have been crazy to think Max would make love to her.

How could she have been so blind as to not recognize the danger *before* asking for his help?

"We have to talk," Max said, sitting next to her on the table.

Annie jerked her legs sideways, away from him. She didn't have many reserves at the moment.

"You were right," he said quietly. "Right about me wanting things to stay the same between us. Ever since you said you were looking for a husband, I've been fighting with myself, knowing I'd lose you if you got married."

"Oh, Max," she whispered, her heart aching. "You won't lose me."

"Everything ends. People fight and go their separate ways. You'll be busy with your new life, and there won't be time for someone like me."

Someone like me...

Annie drew her knees up and wrapped her arms around her legs, hugging them close to her body. "That's why you don't like arguments, you think they end marriages and friendships."

He was silent for a long time. "You don't know what it was like...you never heard the fights. I'd get fond of a new stepparent, a new family. Then there'd be a big fight, and boom it was over. All the promises meant nothing. And nobody ever looked back."

"You did. And the broken promises hurt. They still hurt, don't they?"

Max closed his eyes, but he couldn't hide from Annie. She didn't need to see his eyes, she could see into him, better now than ever. He didn't know why he'd never realized it before, but she was the one person who really understood.

"I wish I could take all that hurt away," Annie whispered. "But I'll always be your friend. It won't ever be over. We might fight and have our problems, but I'm not walking out on you. Fights only end relationships if you want them to."

"I know."

God.

Max rubbed his face. The thick darkness surrounded them like a blanket. How had they gotten to this point? He wanted Annie so much he didn't think the need would ever go away, but knowing it didn't solve anything.

"You're still going out with them, aren't you? McConnell and the sheriff."

"Yes." Two tears trailed down Annie's cheeks. They'd gone through so much, yet nothing had changed. She still wanted to get married, to have a child, and she still had that deadline from the doctor.

"They're lucky men."

Four more tears followed the first two, and she sniffed. "They're not going to *get* lucky, though."

Max made a quiet sound that might have been a laugh. "At least not on the first date, right?"

"Not even to first base."

Letting out a long breath, Max found her hand and threaded their fingers together. "Remember what you said, about missing stuff when you were a teenager?"

Annie nodded. "Yes."

"I think we just covered most of it."

For a moment she didn't understand, then she realized exactly what Max meant. The pain and confusion of young love…. If that's what she'd missed in high school, then it wasn't a great loss.

Of course, there was also the excitement, the breathless anticipation of first kisses. Those were pretty nice.

But the pain of first love wasn't any easier now. It was worse, because she was very much afraid that she loved Max as a woman, and it would take a lot longer than a lifetime to get over that.

Max stood in the doorway of the Mitchell house. It belonged to him, but he didn't feel any triumph at the purchase. Without Annie there it was just a neglected old house.

Sighing, Max sat on the grand staircase and stared at his feet. When had she become so important to him? Was it the day she'd stood on the levee, the light caressing her face, saying how much she wanted a baby?

Was it the night she'd danced in the water and moonlight, her nightgown drenched and clinging to her perfect body?

Or was it the morning he'd first arrived in Mitchellton as an angry boy and she'd brought him a peach pie to say hello? With a sunny smile she'd ignored his surliness, and he'd found himself sitting down, the warm pie between them, devouring it along with a half gallon of ice cream. Laughing for the first time in months.

"Oh...Annie," he murmured, aching clear to his soul.

The cellular phone in his pocket rang. It was the fourth call in the last hour, and he'd ignored the previous three. This time it just kept ringing, pausing for a moment, then starting up again. He considered turning the thing off, maybe by smashing it against a wall, but finally flipped it open.

"What?" he barked into the mike.

"I thought you got a cell phone to be more in touch," scolded his grandmother.

"Sorry," Max said wearily.

"Rough week?"

A vision of Annie rose before his eyes. She surrounded him these days, invading his thoughts, even his dreams when he managed to sleep. Every bite he ate reminded him. He couldn't draw breath without thinking of her.

"Yeah, you could say it was rough."

"Well…just in case it means something to you, Josh Kendrick picked Annie up for their date a little while ago."

Pain slammed through Max, worse than before, and he put a clenched hand on his knee, trying to get through it. He'd known Annie was going out with the sheriff, he just hadn't known what day.

"They're going out to eat, then to that country-western place. Tequila Jack's—the new place on Bailer Road."

Max stood abruptly. "He's taking Annie to a bar?"

"It's not exactly a bar."

"Close enough."

A soft sigh echoed through the phone. "Max, if you don't want Annie, let her be."

"And if I want her?"

There was a long silence before Grace answered. "Then you'd better want it all."

"Marriage and babies and forever," Max said, knowing that's what she meant. "If you're worried

about what I want from Annie, then why are you calling...why tell me about the sheriff?''

''Because you're my grandson and I want you to
be happy. Because I love you more than anyone else
in this world. Because Annie is the woman you were
meant to spend your life with... Are those enough
reasons?''

For a moment Max couldn't talk. ''Meant for me,
huh?'' he said at last. ''You're a coconspirator on her
manhunt. How about that?''

Grace laughed softly. ''I had to do something to
blast you out of your shell. I figured you'd go ballistic
when you found out about the other men...but I never
thought I'd get lucky enough to have Annie ask for
your advice.''

Max wasn't sure luck had any part of it, but then,
maybe it did. Annie wouldn't have asked if he hadn't
shown up with Buffy Blakely. And he wouldn't have
stayed long enough to *be* asked if Tigger hadn't
dropped a mouse on Buffy's foot, making her angry
enough to strand him in Mitchellton.

Mitchellton...he began to smile. Good old Mitchellton. The town he'd thought to escape. Who could
have guessed that he would chase his dreams clear to
Harvard and Boston and back again, only to discover
the end of his rainbow led to the girl next door?

''A country-western bar, huh?''

''Yes, Max. On Bailer Road. You remember where
Bailer Road is, don't you?''

''I remember. I'll talk to you tomorrow, Grandmother.''

''Good luck, dear.''

Max hurried out, only stopping long enough to lock

the door of the house. With any luck he could get to Sacramento, change into something appropriate for a country-western bar and get there ahead of Annie and her sheriff.

He wasn't a country music, two-stepping, mechanical-bull-riding sort of guy, which meant Annie would know that he hadn't shown up by accident.

But he was counting on that.

"Why do I have the feeling I don't have your full attention?" Josh murmured.

Annie looked at the hand he'd extended to help her from the Chevy Blazer and swallowed a sigh. Josh Kendrick was the perfect guy for her. Perfect in every way except one: he wasn't Max.

And all her protests about Max being the wrong man for her boiled down to just one thing: she couldn't ever have him.

"I'm sorry," she whispered.

Josh rested an arm on the open door and raised a quizzical eyebrow. "For being distracted or for something else?"

"Both."

"Let me guess—Max Hunter."

She tried to smile. "Am I that obvious?"

"Actually, it was obvious from the way he watched you during the ice-cream social. He would have strung me up the nearest tree if he could have gotten away with it. I thought he was my real competition— I just hadn't realized he'd already won."

"I'm not a bone under dispute," Annie said dryly. "Besides, Max isn't the jealous type."

"I think he's changed."

"Change isn't Max's strong suit." She put up her chin with a second attempt at a smile. "I'm sorry you wasted an evening with me."

Josh shook his head. "I'm not complaining…and I'm not going anyplace. Who knows what might happen if I stick around long enough? Besides, there's nothing I enjoy better than cheering up a pretty woman."

"Oh, yeah," she said. "That's a lot of fun."

He grinned and put his hand out again. "Come on. I hear this place is getting really popular."

Annie climbed down and looked at the brightly lit country-western bar. She'd never been to Tequila Jack's. It was new, but already had a reputation for good music, good snacks and plenty of dancing. She sincerely hoped Josh wasn't hoping she knew any line dances—she didn't have a clue about dancing, country or otherwise.

The interior was larger than it seemed from outside, and everyone was laughing and having a good time. Despite her flagging spirits, the music got Annie's foot to tapping within a few minutes. She'd just accepted a soda from Josh when she had the strangest feeling of being watched.

Her gaze swept the crowd. She knew a lot of people there, but most everyone was either dancing or looking toward the musicians. The lead singer was crooning a song about the Tennessee River and a mountain band when she saw him sitting along the high bar.

Max.

Dressed in jeans, a faded plaid shirt and scuffed cowboy boots, with a cowboy hat drawn low over his forehead. He blended with the friendly crowd, though there wasn't another man so wickedly attractive.

A smile curved Max's mouth when their eyes met, and he lifted his glass in a silent toast.

It hurt.

And it made her furious.

Max was about as country as a magnum of champagne. She didn't know how he'd learned they were coming to Tequila Jack's, but she *did* know he was making this even harder for her. They would always be friends, but she had to get him out of her heart, or it would tear her into pieces.

Josh touched her arm. "Annie, is something wrong?"

"Yes. It's Max," she muttered, her mouth straight with anger.

"So it is."

"I don't know how he found out where we were going, but he did. Get ready to arrest me, sheriff, because I'm going to strangle him."

"He found out because I told Grace Hunter and suggested she give her grandson a call," Josh said calmly, taking a swig of light beer. He rolled the edge of his bottle on the table, watching bubbles rise in the amber liquid.

"You…*what?*"

"I told Mrs. Hunter. Actually, she probably would have called him without the suggestion, but I wanted to be sure."

Annie swallowed and tried counting to ten. "Why did you want Max to know where we were going?"

"Well…" Josh sat back and shrugged. "I like you,

so I wanted to find out how serious things were with the guy. It looks as if I have my answer.''

"Max being here doesn't mean anything.''

"No?''

God save her from men who thought they knew everything. Annie put her drink on the table so hard it slopped over the sides. "Forget it. I'll be back in a minute...after I kill him. Where's your gun?''

"I thought you were using strangulation.''

"No, I'm saving that for you,'' she snapped, getting up and marching toward Max. But she wasn't angry with Josh, not really. It was Max Hunter who was making her crazy.

"Hey, Annie,'' Max said, tipping his cowboy hat back on his head.

"Don't 'hey' me,'' she growled. "You followed us.''

"To be absolutely accurate, I got here ahead of you.''

"Outside,'' she said, flipping her thumb in the direction of the door.

"Yes, ma'am.''

Annie could have sworn there was a gleam of anticipation in Max's dark eyes, but she was angry and hurt, and she couldn't spare the energy to wonder what he was thinking about.

All was fair in love and war, and this was definitely war!

Chapter Ten

"What are you doing?" Annie demanded the minute they were alone outside. "I thought we…cleared this up. On Saturday," she said, unable to say more for fear of crying.

"I changed my mind."

She glared. *Men.* And they said women couldn't make up their minds. "I can't believe you came here."

"Believe it, sweetheart."

"I told you not to call me that."

"Actually," Max said, a smile playing on his mouth, "you told me not to call you honey. That leaves a lot of territory in between."

"You know exactly what I meant. I said to just call me Annie."

His head shook. "Nope, no way. You aren't 'just' anything. I can't let you say something like that."

"*Jeez.*"

She gave him a dark look that promised dire retribution. Not that she'd be able to follow through, because she was weak when it came to Max. Mostly weak in the head. Otherwise she would have been smart enough to stay away from him and to keep her romantic woes private.

Romantic guidance counselor.

Annie practically snorted. She would have been safer taking advice from Barnard. Barnard didn't make her heart beat fast. He didn't act jealous when he couldn't possibly *be* jealous. And he was twelve pounds of cuddly charm. Max wasn't cuddly, he was hard and dangerous and exciting.

"You're upset," Max murmured. "I understand."

"That's right, you're so understanding. About everything."

His mouth tightened, and she could have sworn her snide remark had hit an unexpected target. "Sorry," she whispered. "You didn't deserve that."

Despite the darkness in Max's face, he shook his head. "Yes, I did. But there's one thing *you* don't understand. You objected the other night when I said you were my best friend, but you are. We may not talk about things the way we should—about important things—but there's no one I trust more."

Darn him. How could she stay angry when he was being so earnest and sincere? "I wish you wouldn't say stuff like that," she said crossly. "You came and spied on my date. I'm not ready to forgive you."

"So say it," he drawled.

"Say what?"

"Whatever you want."

She didn't have the slightest notion what had gotten

into Max, but she wasn't playing along. "I'm going back inside and asking Josh to take me someplace else. Don't follow. Don't ask where we're going. Just go home."

"Josh isn't taking you anywhere."

"Why are you doing this?" she said, her voice rising. "You don't want me, but you don't want anyone else to have me, either."

"Okay, that's fair enough. I can see how it would look like that." Max leaned against his BMW, lifted one leg and wiggled the toe of his cowboy boot. "Anything else?"

"What else?" she asked impatiently.

"Anything else you want to get off your chest? Go ahead," he prompted. "Let me have it."

"You're impossible," she hissed.

"I know. But I'm listening."

Annie's eyes narrowed as she realized Max was baiting her. Starting a fight. Inviting her to let go and have at him, and she didn't stop to question why.

"All right," she snapped. "I'm sorry that your mother and father were such a loss at being parents. I'm sorry they hurt you, but you keep forgetting that Grace never let you down, that no matter how many stupid stunts you pulled, she never stopped loving you. Never once."

"Can't argue that one." His amiable tone threw Annie for a moment.

"Y-yes." She drew a breath, still charged with adrenaline. "You're so busy making sure nobody leaves you again you don't let anyone get close, period. People makes choices, Max, and your parents made terrible ones. They didn't make commitments, they had temporary living arrangements with a marriage certificate. But that's them, not you. Their decisions don't have to affect your entire life.''

''That's for sure.''

''Stop agreeing with me!''

Max scratched his jaw. He didn't look the least bit upset, more amused, and it infuriated her. ''I'm new to this fighting stuff. You mean I can't agree that you're right, even when you are?''

''I...'' Annie shook her head with a rueful laugh. She was being unreasonable, but she'd never expected Max to be so calm about it. He'd never liked the ''emotional crap,'' as he'd so succinctly put it when they were kids.

''Come here,'' Max urged, holding out his hand.

She hesitated, then shrugged. They couldn't get into much trouble in the parking lot—too much potential for an audience. His strong hands fastened around her waist, and he lifted her to the hood of his car, settling her gently, his fingers lingering for a moment.

''What's going on, Max?'' she asked softly. ''Did you fall down? Get hit by a train? Maybe I should rush you to a doctor to see if you've got a concussion or something.''

He smiled. ''Why, because I'm not running for hills over a little disagreement?''

''Something like that.'' Annie smoothed the soft fabric of her skirt, waiting for more. When he didn't say anything right away she sneaked a peek from under her lashes. ''Have you been kidnapped and replaced by aliens?'' she ventured. ''Is the real Max Hunter on his way to Mars?''

"Nope, it's the real me."

Max looked at Annie and thought his heart would burst, he loved her so much. She sat on his car, her hair soft around her face, a pretty dress framing her petite beauty, and she glowed with feminine poise.

He wanted to propose, but was afraid she'd take a good hard look at him and realize she could have any man. Why should she take a guy who'd made a career of avoiding emotional commitments?

"Uh, I have some news," he said.

"I see. You followed me on the first real date of my life so you could tell me something."

"It wasn't your first date," he corrected. "Technically the carnival was your first real date. I'm not counting dinner in Old Sacramento. I screwed that one up."

"You're splitting hairs."

From the corner of his eye Max saw Josh Kendrick watching them from a window. He returned the challenging stare. He'd never been the possessive sort before, but that was before he'd realized he had something worth keeping.

Too late, Max wanted to say.

It wasn't politically correct, but since the day nine-year-old Annie had appeared at the door with that fresh peach pie, she'd belonged to him. Just because he'd been too blind and stubborn to understand, it shouldn't mean he didn't have a chance now.

Josh turned away, though not before Max saw a wry smile on the other man's face. They understood each other pretty well, all things considered.

"What's your good news?" Annie prompted.

Max took off his hat and balanced it on his hand.

It was one thing to decide he'd be more open, another thing to follow through. "I bought the Mitchell House. It still has to go through escrow, but we signed the papers this afternoon and I don't expect any problems."

"That's…nice."

"It's going to need a lot of work. And, uh, you did say you'd help."

She shook her head. "So you had to make sure I'd follow through on my promise. That's a lousy excuse for showing up here, Max, and you know it."

"I wasn't worried about your promise. But you were so upset about the idea of someone tearing it down, I thought you'd appreciate knowing the place was safe."

"Okay. So you bought the Mitchell house and are going to make tons of money on it. Now may I go back inside and finish my date?"

"It's not an investment. I'm going to live there," Max said quietly. "With my wife."

For a second Annie felt as if she'd been slapped, then she looked at Max, trying not to jump to conclusions. "Your…wife?" she asked carefully. "I didn't even know you were engaged."

"No reason you should. I haven't asked her yet."

Annie's heart seemed to stop, then raced ahead so quickly she was in danger of passing out. Max had been acting very strangely the past couple of weeks; it didn't mean anything that he was buying a house and talking about marriage. He might have found the perfect ice queen and was planning to pop the question the next time she thawed.

"What's keeping you? From…asking?"

"We've had a little trouble," he murmured. "I didn't mean to hurt her, but I did. Now I'm not sure she'll want to marry me and have a baby together."

"Then she must be crazy."

"Mmm, no." Max stroked her cheek. "She's the sweetest, dearest woman I've ever known. She probably has too much sense to marry a dope like me, but I'll still do my to convince her."

"You aren't a dope, Max."

"Thank you. That's very generous."

Annie looked down at her hands, clenched tightly in her lap. She wanted to hear him propose, and she was afraid that he would. It didn't make sense, but love wasn't terribly logical. Especially when she didn't know why Max would suddenly decide he wanted to join an institution he'd disparaged for years.

"What do you think she'll say, Annie?" Max asked, caressing the back of her neck. "Is she going to give me a chance, or will she decide I've hurt her too much?"

"I'm sure she'll forgive you…if she loves you."

"I hope you're right." Max kissed the corner of Annie's mouth. "Because I can't sleep for thinking about her. I want to spend the rest of my life holding her through the night, showing her what she does to me. Being there when she needs to cry and laugh and talk about anything…and everything."

"Fighting?"

He smiled. "I'm sure we'll fight. But a wise person once told me that fighting only has to end a relationship if you want it to, so I'm not worried about it any longer. I'd never do anything to lose her, and I know if she makes a promise to me, she'll keep it."

"Max," she moaned. "You don't believe in marriage. You think it's nothing more than a temporary arrangement. How could you have changed your mind so quickly?"

"I wouldn't say it was *quickly*. It took me over twenty-two years to get to this point," he said, stroking strands of hair from her forehead. "I realize that's a long time. But some things just take a while. And I'm pretty hardheaded, at least that's what Grandmother says."

"Three weeks ago you were very clear about your feelings," Annie said painfully. "Let's see...you said all the women you knew were batty about the subject of marriage. And you asked if we'd joined a club."

Damn. Max had known some of his words would come back to haunt him. Over the years he'd said plenty about love and marriage, none of it too flattering. Mitchellton was going to have a huge belly laugh over his change of heart. But they could laugh all they wanted, because he'd be smiling, too, as long as Annie was standing next to him.

"That was my last gasp," he promised. "My last protest and a stupid one, at that."

Annie bit her lip. "But kids. You never wanted them."

Max bent closer, a hand on her waist, the other stroking her hair. The warmth and tenderness in his touch nearly made her cry. "I didn't want a child who would become a prize to fight over in a divorce. I never wanted a child of mine to go through that kind of unhappiness, so it was just easier to say I didn't want a family.''

A cool breeze ruffled Annie's skirt, and she traced the light floral print with the tip of a finger. She wanted to believe so very much, but that same desire made her cautious.

''It's a big step,'' she said. ''Going from bachelor to married man and father so quickly.''

And I need to get pregnant right away. Annie swallowed, still waiting. Still hoping.

Max pulled her against him. ''Not if it's with the right woman. I love you so much, Annie. I'm not sure when it started, probably when we were kids and you were so sweet and kind. It took the possibility of losing you to make me realize what I should have known all along.''

She didn't say anything for a long time. ''What if I can't even have one baby?'' she whispered, and Max knew it was the fear that had lingered, deep in her heart, ever since the doctor had discovered she would have to have surgery.

''I just need to know that you love me,'' he said softly. ''Having a baby should come from two people loving with everything they've got. The only guarantee I can offer is that if it doesn't happen, if we never have a child, the loving won't change.''

Tears spilled down Annie's cheeks, and she looked up. Truth blazed in Max's eyes, and an inarticulate cry escaped from her throat. He'd told her once that the right man wouldn't care whether she could have children or not, but neither one of them had realized he was talking about himself.

''I love you, too,'' she said shakily.

"Annie..." He swept her close, raining kisses on her face, trying to wipe the tears away. "Don't, baby," he pleaded. "Don't cry."

"I'm just happy."

Max drew back to be sure, searching her face. "Thank God for that."

With a joyful laugh he lifted Annie in his arms and whirled with her around the parking lot. Love was the freedom he'd never known, the excitement he'd searched for his entire life.

"Max, put me down," Annie scolded.

"Not a chance." He kissed the tip of her nose and, without missing a beat, carried her toward the front door of Tequila Jack's. One of the patrons held it open while he walked inside, holding her against his heart.

"Well, if it isn't that good ol' boy, Max Hunter," said the lead singer of the band.

Max looked more closely and realized it was one of his friends from high school. "Hi, Conn. Yup, it's me. How've you been?"

"Pretty good."

There were a lot of familiar faces in the crowd, and Max's smile broadened.

Perfect.

"Josh," he called, and the sheriff pushed his way to the front. "Still that got that cell phone?"

Josh pulled it out, a half smile on his face. "All things considered, I really shouldn't do this," he said. "But I will for Annie."

"For Annie, then. Dial my grandmother, will you?" Max reeled off the number while the other man pressed the buttons.

Their curious audience edged closer.

"Max, what are you doing?" Annie asked.

"Taking care of business…family business." Max sat on one of the sturdy tables and arranged her across his legs. He accepted the phone and put it against his ear. "Grandmother? It's me. We just wanted you to be the first to know…Annie and I are getting married."

Grace's cry of pleasure was drowned out by a roar from the crowd, congratulations and drumrolls from the band. Folks surged forward, and Max lost track of the phone as it went from friend to friend so they could share the moment with his grandmother. Hands clapped him on the back and tried to snatch Annie away, but he held her close.

"One of the mighty has fallen," someone declared over the loudspeaker.

Max looked down at Annie. Her face was shining with happiness. "I fell, all right. All the away," he whispered, for her ears only. "Love is the sweetest fall of all."

Epilogue

"Happy, darling?"

Annie smiled dreamily and leaned against her husband's chest, his strong arms encircling her.

"Mmm. I love the fireflies," she said, watching the flickers of ghostly light spark across the wide expanse of the Mississippi River and on the dark shore.

Max's chuckle rumbled through her. "I know. That's all you talked about when we got back from our honeymoon. I swear, everyone thought lightning bugs were the only thing you saw the entire trip."

"It almost was...except for the inside of our cabin."

His laugh was louder this time. "And whose fault was that?"

"Mine. But I didn't hear you complaining."

"How could I complain about something so close to my heart?" Max whispered. His breath curled into Annie's ear, sending sensual shivers throughout her body. They knew each other so well now, knew the rhythms of their lovemaking, knew what pleasured the most, but there were always sweet surprises waiting.

It was quieter on this part of the deck, away from the chattering of tourists and the hum of the paddle wheel. The hushed music of the river resonated through Annie, and she closed her eyes, drifting with the night. The past two years had been so hectic that it was nice to have a tranquil moment to enjoy the night and the man who stood so close, holding her.

They'd decided to make a trip to the Mississippi an annual event. Between family and work it wouldn't always be easy to get away from Mitchellton, but they'd made a commitment to each other. And this year had been much easier to plan than the last. Quieter, too.

"What are you thinking about?" Max asked.

Annie grinned. "That the crew and other passengers must be glad we left the twins at home this trip."

Max put his head back and laughed. "They weren't that loud."

"Yes, they were." She dearly loved her two sons and took joy in their healthy lungs, but she was honest: most people preferred sleeping more than forty-five minutes at a stretch. "We're lucky to have Grace as a baby-sitter."

"Grandmother says she's the lucky one. She'd keep them forever if we'd let her."

Max crossed his arms more closely around her, and Annie thought about the precious secret resting beneath his strong hands. He didn't know; she still hadn't found the way to tell him they were going to have another child. A miracle, like the rest of their life together.

Annie turned and put her cheek against her husband's heart. His steadily increasing pulse told her he was becoming aroused.

"Mmm," she murmured again, her body softening with the same sweet ache.

It wouldn't be long before they sought the privacy of their cabin. No matter how often they held each other, they could never get enough. Max often declared, half-teasing, half-serious, they would have to spend the rest of their lives making up for lost time.

"And I have to admit a second honeymoon is more romantic without a pair of two-month-old babies sleeping in the same room," she said.

Max smiled, though he remembered some very romantic moments stolen between wiping up splashed bathwater, changing diapers and hungry babies nursing at Annie's breast. He loved seeing their sons cuddled against her…loved the gentle tenderness she showered on her entire family. There couldn't be a soul in Mitchellton who didn't know he was the luckiest man ever born.

Mitchellton…he shook his head with rueful humor.

Who would have guessed he'd come full circle, enjoying that little town after all this time?

They'd returned from their honeymoon, prepared to do battle on the Mitchell—now Hunter—House, only to find their friends and neighbors showing up, helping to clean and make it habitable. Beneath the grime of decades the house proved to be in better condition that he'd expected, though there was plenty of work left to be done.

Ducking his head, Max kissed the soft curve of Annie's neck. He drew a breath, infusing his senses with her fragrance. She was so warm and enticing. His need for her had built all evening, through the candlelight dinner, the music playing and the slow stroll on the deck. He couldn't wait much longer.

He wasn't the patient sort—not when it came to loving his wife—but there was something to be said for anticipation. *Sometimes.* And he knew how much she enjoyed watching the fireflies dance on the water's edge.

"Sweetheart, do you want a lesson on how those bugs get their lightning?" he teased.

"You and your 'lessons,'" Annie scolded, but she wasn't angry. She bit lightly through Max's shirt, testing the flat nipple she'd discovered.

"No?" His hips thrust toward her, speaking a language as instinctive and old as time and the river.

"No." Annie smoothed her cheek on his chest, knowing she was both soothing and exciting her husband. "I know all I need to know about lightning bugs."

Scientists could explain until they were blue in the face about fireflies and how they made the light, but it was still magical...as magical and mysterious as the way two people could be incomplete until they were joined.

Annie slid her arms around Max's neck, and they swayed together. There wasn't any doubt about the level of his urgency: it pressed into her tummy, unyielding and exciting, and she thought again about the baby.

Her being able to conceive a second time was

against all odds. She'd had her surgery after twins were born, and the surgeon had warned them, once more, not to get their hopes up. The extent of the surgery and the inevitable scar tissue made it unlikely she would have another child.

Annie shook with a silent laugh. The surgeon obviously hadn't counted on her husband's virility.

"Sweetheart?" Max's voice was strained, his fingers seeking her more intimate curves. "Have you seen enough lightning for one night?"

"I don't know. Let's go make some in our cabin, just in case," she whispered.

With a hot smile Max took her hand and hurried down the deck until they were running. The steward was in their cabin, turning down the covers, when they burst inside. The poor man took one look at their flushed faces and sprinted out the door.

Max tumbled backward on the bed, laughing, holding Annie close to him. "I love you," he said, turning with her in his arms. "Don't ever forget that."

"Just keep telling me."

"No problem." He slid tiny buttons from their holes, steadily uncovering the feminine curves beneath his wife's dress. "That's one lesson I won't forget."

It hadn't been easy opening up, talking about the things that had always made him uncomfortable, especially in the beginning. Even to Annie. But in time he'd learned how to talk with her about the things that really mattered. And her patience with his occasional lapses never ceased to amaze him.

"Lovely," he whispered, nuzzling the creamy breast he'd freed from a lacy bra.

An eager nipple begged for attention, and Max drew it into his mouth, delighted with the swift breath of air she took. His fingers swept the remaining clothes from Annie's body, and after an endless moment of tasting her, he lifted his head.

The light from the bedside table fell across them, and he flexed his hand on her shoulder. The contrast between the peach satin of Annie's skin and his dark-bronze flesh still fascinated him. He supposed it always would.

A few months before she'd suggested they learn more about his Apache heritage so they could share it with their sons. The memory of her radiant eyes, the pride she took in every part of him, made his heart swell.

"Max..."

"Yes?"

"You're way overdressed for this occasion."

He blinked, realizing that he'd been so anxious to gain access to Annie's sweet curves he'd neglected to do more than kick off his shoes.

Smiling, Annie slid her fingers into the space between the buttons on Max's shirt, seeking the rigid muscles beneath. She tugged the tails from his jeans and smoothed her palms over his hard stomach. When his clothes lay on the floor along with hers, she shook her hair over his hips and heard a harsh groan.

Annie's smile was hidden by the veils of her hair. The first time she'd done this to Max, his reaction had alarmed her.

Did I hurt you? she'd asked anxiously.

Yes, he'd growled. With the most exquisite kind of pain.

She understood now...and treated her husband to more of the sensual torment until he took control, his hands already all over her, and rolled her beneath him.

Hot and hard, he pressed into her softness. Annie moaned, her hips bucking in response. And it did seem as if lightning swept the room, illuminating every dark place, every hidden corner. The tension built and built until she heard the words in her ears, the urgent words she'd been waiting for.

"Now, baby, *now.*"

After two years she was attuned to his loving, and she let herself fly, spinning away into the lightning-shattered darkness, right along with Max.

Much later Annie floated back into herself while Max held her and breathed in short, harsh gasps. She rested her cheek on his shoulder, knowing the quiet moment wouldn't last. This was one of those nights when they couldn't get enough.

He swept his fingers down her body, caressing the curve of her hip, then found her breasts again.

"You still haven't gained back all the weight the doctor ordered," he murmured, teasing the tips. "Some, but you lost too much nursing the twins."

Annie held her breath. Max nagged her about those pounds the doctor insisted she needed, but the new fullness of her breasts was from pregnancy, not the nutritional supplements he kept making her drink.

"Uh, I'll probably gain a bit in the next few months," she said. She couldn't keep from smiling, anticipating her husband's reaction to the news.

"You should have gained more before now," he grumbled.

"Maybe, but I wasn't pregnant before."

Max froze.

He could swear his wife had just said she was pregnant. There was a stillness in the room, in Annie's body, and he twisted to look in her face.

"Annie?"

She nodded, her eyes shining like the sun.

"Oh, my." Max laughed out of the sheer joy of living and of being with the one person in the world who could make him this happy. "How? I don't understand? It's incredible," he said, his thrilled words spilling over each other.

"I'm not sure…but I don't think the doctor calculated how potent you are," Annie said.

Max looked in her lovely eyes, and they shared a long smile. What they had together was pure, heaven-sent magic, and they wouldn't question the gift.

But they'd cherish it for the rest of their lives.

*   *   *   *   *

Feel like a star with Silhouette.

We will fly you and a guest to New York City for an exciting weekend stay at a glamorous 5-star hotel. Experience a refreshing day at one of New York's trendiest spas and have your photo taken by a professional. Plus, receive $1,000 U.S. spending money!

Flowers...long walks...dinner for two... how does Silhouette Books make romance come alive for you?

Send us a script, with 500 words or less, along with visuals (only drawings, magazine cutouts or photographs or combination thereof). Show us how Silhouette Makes Your Love Come Alive. Be creative and have fun. No purchase necessary. All entries must be clearly marked with your name, address and telephone number. All entries will become property of Silhouette and are not returnable. **Contest closes September 28, 2001.**

Please send your entry to: **Silhouette Makes You a Star!**

Look for contest details on the next page, by visiting www.eHarlequin.com or request a copy by sending a self-addressed envelope to the applicable address above. Contest open to Canadian and U.S. residents who are 18 or over. Void where prohibited.

Our lucky winner's photo will appear in a Silhouette ad. Join the fun!

HARLEQUIN "SILHOUETTE MAKES YOU A STAR!" CONTEST 1308
OFFICIAL RULES
NO PURCHASE NECESSARY TO ENTER

1. To enter, follow directions published in the offer to which you are responding. Contest begins June 1, 2001, and ends on September 28, 2001. Entries must be postmarked by September 28, 2001, and received by October 5, 2001. Enter by hand-printing (or typing) on an 8 ½" x 11" piece of paper your name, address (including zip code), contest number/name and attaching a script containing 500 words or less, along with drawings, photographs or magazine cutouts, or combinations thereof (i.e., collage) on no larger than 9" x 12" piece of paper, describing how the Silhouette books make romance come alive for you. Mail via first-class mail to: Harlequin "Silhouette Makes You a Star!" Contest 1308, (in the U.S.) P.O. Box 9069, Buffalo, NY 14269-9069, (in Canada) P.O. Box 637, Fort Erie, Ontario, Canada L2A 5X3. Limit one entry per person, household or organization.

2. Contests will be judged by a panel of members of the Harlequin editorial, marketing and public relations staff. Fifty percent of criteria will be judged against script and fifty percent will be judged against drawing, photographs and/or magazine cutouts. Judging criteria will be based on the following:

   - Sincerity—25%
   - Originality and Creativity—50%
   - Emotionally Compelling—25%

   In the event of a tie, duplicate prizes will be awarded. Decisions of the judges are final.

3. All entries become the property of Torstar Corp. and may be used for future promotional purposes. Entries will not be returned. No responsibility is assumed for lost, late, illegible, incomplete, inaccurate, nondelivered or misdirected mail.

4. Contest open only to residents of the U.S. (except Puerto Rico) and Canada who are 18 years of age or older, and is void wherever prohibited by law; all applicable laws and regulations apply. Any litigation within the Province of Quebec respecting the conduct or organization of a publicity contest may be submitted to the Régie des alcools, des courses et des jeux for a ruling. Any litigation respecting the awarding of a prize may be submitted to the Régie des alcools, des courses et des jeux only for the purpose of helping the parties reach a settlement. Employees and immediate family members of Torstar Corp. and D. L. Blair, Inc., their affiliates, subsidiaries and all other agencies, entities and persons connected with the use, marketing or conduct of this contest are not eligible to enter. Taxes on prizes are the sole responsibility of the winner. Acceptance of any prize offered constitutes permission to use winner's name, photograph or other likeness for the purposes of advertising, trade and promotion on behalf of Torstar Corp., its affiliates and subsidiaries without further compensation to the winner, unless prohibited by law.

5. Winner will be determined no later than November 30, 2001, and will be notified by mail. Winner will be required to sign and return an Affidavit of Eligibility/Release of Liability/Publicity Release form within 15 days after winner notification. Noncompliance within that time period may result in disqualification and an alternative winner may be selected. All travelers must execute a Release of Liability prior to ticketing and must possess required travel documents (e.g., passport, photo ID) where applicable. Trip must be booked by December 31, 2001, and completed within one year of notification. No substitution of prize permitted by winner. Torstar Corp. and D. L. Blair, Inc., their parents, affiliates and subsidiaries are not responsible for errors in printing of contest, entries and/or game pieces. In the event of printing or other errors that may result in unintended prize values or duplication of prizes, all affected game pieces or entries shall be null and void. **Purchase or acceptance of a product offer does not improve your chances of winning.**

6. Prizes: (1) Grand Prize—A 2-night/3-day trip for two (2) to New York City, including round-trip coach air transportation nearest winner's home and hotel accommodations (double occupancy) at The Plaza Hotel, a glamorous afternoon makeover at a trendy New York spa, $1,000 in U.S. spending money and an opportunity to have a professional photo taken and appear in a Silhouette advertisement (approximate retail value: $7,000). (10) Ten Runner-Up Prizes of gift packages (retail value $50 ea.). Prizes consist of only those items listed as part of the prize. Limit one prize per person. Prize is valued in U.S. currency.

7. For the name of the winner (available after December 31, 2001) send a self-addressed, stamped envelope to: Harlequin "Silhouette Makes You a Star!" Contest 1197 Winners, P.O. Box 4200 Blair, NE 68009-4200 or you may access the www.eHarlequin.com Web site through February 28, 2002.

Contest sponsored by Torstar Corp., P.O. Box 9042, Buffalo, NY 14269-9042.

SRMYAS2

If you enjoyed what you just read,
then we've got an offer you can't resist!

Take 2 bestselling love stories FREE!

Plus get a FREE surprise gift!

MAITLAND MATERNITY

**You loved
the Maitland
family. Now meet
the long-lost Maitlands...!**

In August 2001, Marie Ferrarella introduces
Rafe Maitland, a rugged rancher with a little girl he'd
do anything to keep, including—*gulp!*—get married,
in **THE INHERITANCE**, a specially packaged story!

Look for it near Silhouette and Harlequin's single titles!

**Then meet Rafe's siblings in
Silhouette Romance® in the coming months:**

Myrna Mackenzie continues the story
of the Maitlands with prodigal
daughter Laura Maitland in
September 2001's
A VERY SPECIAL DELIVERY.

October 2001 brings
the conclusion to this
spin-off of the popular
Maitland family series, reuniting
black sheep Luke Maitland with
his family in Stella Bagwell's
THE MISSING MAITLAND.

Available at your favorite retail outlet.

Silhouette®
Where love comes alive™